'What, you think that pressing letters is somehow going to open this door?' Paz gave Podkin a scornful look as she shoved Pook up to the door handle. His fingers started tracing the symbols and pushing them here and there, making a series of clicking sounds.

'Just watch,' said Podkin. He folded his arms and gave Paz his best smug smile.

'There's ten stones there, Podkin. There must be millions of different combinations. There's absolutely no way—'

She was interrupted by a loud *clank*, and the door began to swing inwards with a deep grinding sound . . .

ABOUT THE AUTHOR

Kieran Larwood has been passionate about stories and storytelling ever since reading *The Hobbit* age six. He graduated from Southampton University with a degree in English Literature and worked as a Reception teacher in a primary school. He now writes full-time. He lives on the Isle of Wight with his family, and between work, fatherhood and writing doesn't get nearly enough sleep.

ABOUT THE ILLUSTRATOR

David Wyatt lives in Devon. He has illustrated many novels but is also much admired for his concept and character work. He has illustrated tales by a number of high-profile fantasy authors such as Diana Wynne Jones, Terry Pratchett, Philip Pullman and J. R. R. Tolkien.

THE GIFT OF
DARK
HOLLOW

KIERAN LARWOOD

ILLUSTRATED BY DAVID WYATT

FABER & FABER

First published in 2017
by Faber & Faber Limited
Bloomsbury House,
74–77 Great Russell Street,
London WC1B 3DA
This paperback edition first published in 2018

Typeset by M Rules
Printed by CPI Group (UK) Ltd, Croydon CR0 4YY
All rights reserved
Text and Maps © Kieran Larwood, 2017
Interior Illustrations © David Wyatt, 2017
Cover Illustration © Fernando Juarez, 2017

The right of Kieran Larwood and David Wyatt to be identified as
author and illustrator of this work respectively has been asserted
in accordance with Section 77 of the Copyright, Designs and
Patents Act 1988

A CIP record for this book
is available from the British Library

ISBN 978–0–571–32842–0

FSC
www.fsc.org
MIX
Paper from
responsible sources
FSC® C020471

For Eli

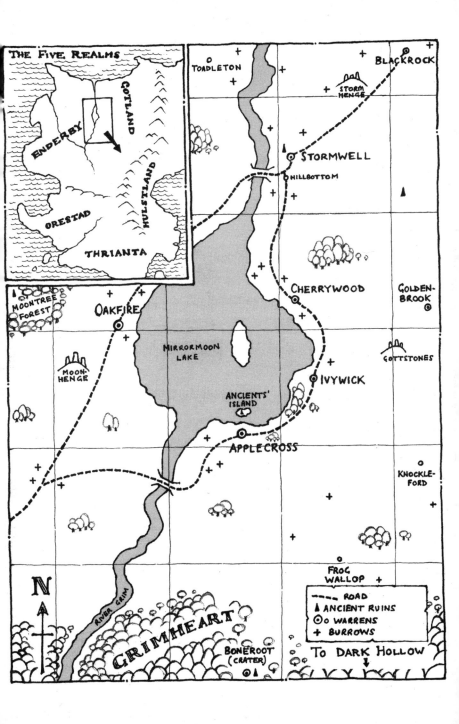

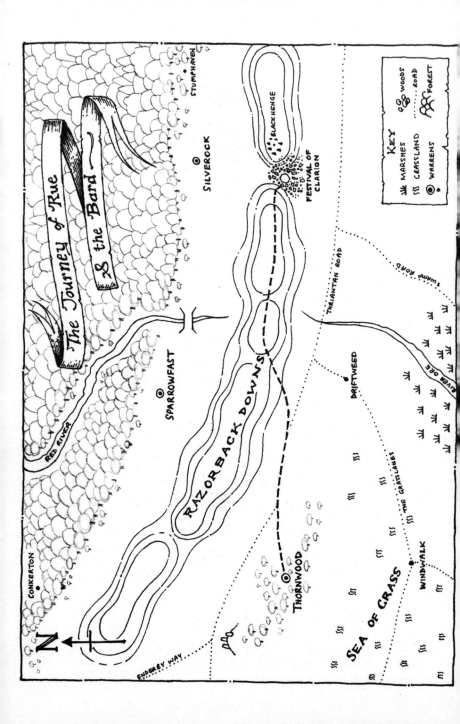

Prologue

He still dreams about them sometimes. Nightmares that leave him wide-eyed and gasping, with fears sixty years old pounding fresh through his blood.

It is never the Gorm themselves, strangely enough. Those hulking, clanking monsters of iron and flesh with their blank red eyes. Anyone would think they would be the things to haunt him all the way to old age.

No. It's always the crows that plague his sleep. The mindless servants of the Gorm. Simple birds,

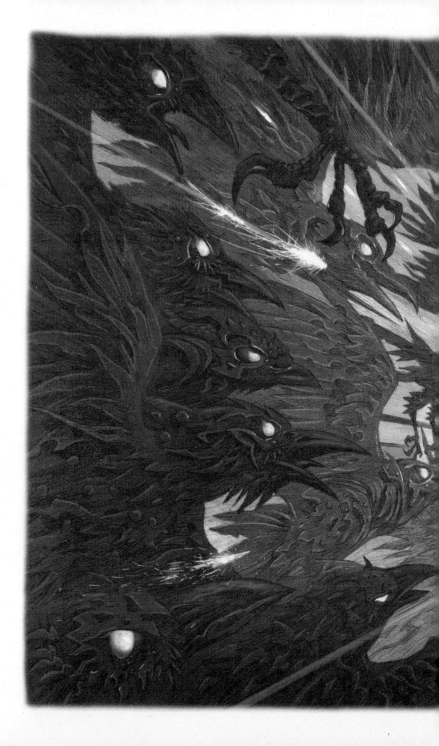

twisted by magic into jagged, flapping things with bladed beaks and torn iron feathers.

He sees them gathering in dark skies: swarms of them circling in a clashing, crashing mass of metal, cawing and screeching to each other in a chorus like a thousand hammers pounding on a thousand anvils.

They wheel and spin, striking sparks off each other as their wings touch, and he stands – a small rabbit once again – staring up at them, praying they don't spot him alone and helpless on the wide open ground below.

But they always do.

One red eye at first, glaring at him from the throng. A single crow shrieks with horrible joy and peels off from its brothers and sisters, flapping towards him, making all the others turn and stare, their hungry, hungry beaks like razor-sharp shears . . .

And on a good night, that's when he wakes up.

CHAPTER ONE

Cuckoo

Thornwood warren is still sleeping as the bard tiptoes out of his room, the crow-dream still echoing in his head, making him twitch at imaginary creaks of iron wings.

The longburrow is empty but for the slumped shape of one lazy rabbit, snoring with his head on a table; an empty mead jug and a pool of dribble in front of him. The fire is quietly smouldering, giving the place a dim orange glow as the bard pads silently past. He wraps his cloak about him and heads up the draughty entrance tunnel.

At the doorway, the usual guard, huge and annoying, is asleep at his post, blowing bubbles and twitching his ears as he dreams away to himself. Making a mental note to report him to Chief Hubert, the bard steps around him and opens one of the broad oak doors a crack – just enough to slip outside.

It is moments before dawn, and the brightening sky peeps out between the bare branches of the trees above. The snow has all but vanished from the ground, and here and there the bard can see a brave daffodil or snowdrop pushing its head out of the cold hard ground to greet the coming spring. He follows the path between the trees, out to the edge of the Thornwood, where he can see the spine of the Razorback downs stretching away to the east. A blanket of mist is draped across the valley, and the line of hills looks like a giant serpent, wriggling its way through a pale, smoky sea.

The bard stands and stares, breathing in the fresh new scents of the season. Soon, crinkly green leaves will be bursting from the branches all around, blazing away the last of winter with their bright living colours.

Time for me to be on the move again, he thinks. It is not often he stays in one place for three months (and there are reasons it isn't safe to do so) but it also isn't often that he sees his older brother.

Podkin. The bard sighs. It will be a shame to leave him. To every other rabbit in the warren, he is just an old longbeard. A retired warrior, sitting in the longburrow corner every night, playing Foxpaw with the other veterans and dozing. If only they knew . . .

A twig snaps somewhere on the path behind, and the bard suddenly stops his dreaming. Tiny paws patter, and there is a rustle as something hides behind a bush.

'You might as well come out,' calls the bard. 'You're about as stealthy as an overweight badger with granite clogs on.'

The bush rustles again, and a small figure steps out, all huge floppy ears and brown speckled fur. It is one of the chieftain's sons: the little lad who sits and listens to the bard's tales so intently every night, chipping in with vivid observations and difficult questions. 'The sensible rabbit', the bard always thinks of him, although he has learnt that his name is actually Rue.

'Sorry, sir,' Rue says, eyes on the ground. 'I wasn't spying on you, just . . .'

'Sneaking up behind me and watching what I was doing? I believe that is the *actual definition* of spying.'

'Yes, sir. Sorry, sir.' The little rabbit looks as though he is about to cry. He has mentioned several hundred times how much he wants to become a bard, and now he probably thinks he has ruined his chances. The bard takes pity on him.

'Oh, whiskers I wasn't doing anything worth spying on, anyway. What I *would* like to know is how you managed to spot me coming out here at this time of the morning. Shouldn't you be tucked up in your burrow, asleep?'

'I couldn't sleep, sir. I've got six brothers in my bed, and they all snore so much, it keeps me awake. I was under one of the tables in the longburrow, practising some of my tales, and I saw you walking past. I wondered if you might be doing something . . . bardy. So I followed you. I really *would* like to become a bard, sir.'

'So you've told me. At least half a million times. And stop calling me "sir". I'm not a chieftain or a knight. Just an old, tired storyteller.' The bard pulls at his beard, wondering how much to encourage the little rabbit. If he's awful at storytelling then there'll have to be a very awkward conversation. And if he isn't? All bards know there is a duty to train up newcomers with potential. And who will that fall on? *It can't be me*, the bard thinks. *Not now, with things as they are . . .*

The bard notices Rue is still blinking up at him, the tender light of hope in his eyes. He's left it far too long to just say 'go away' and be done with it now. He'll have to do or say something. Preferably something encouraging.

A little test then. Just like the bard's old master gave to him. He wanders over to a fallen tree and makes himself comfortable amongst the moss and mushrooms. Rue follows, his huge brown eyes drinking in the bard's every move. For a moment they stare at each other, and then the bard nods to himself.

'Very well, little one,' he says. 'Let's see what you've got. Why don't you tell me a tale?'

'A tale? Here? Now?' Rue's ears begin to shake. He has never imagined actually *telling* someone one of his stories, let alone the bard himself.

'Yes, on you go.' The bard's eyes twinkle. 'The Tale of the Twelve Gifts would be a good one. You've heard me tell it at least five times this winter.'

Rue gulps. He breathes deeply. He reaches into his mind for the story, and begins to unravel it.

'Well. It was a long time ago, see? I mean a long, *long* time ago. Back when the world was new and memories hadn't even begun.'

Rue looks at the bard for approval, but his face gives nothing away. Rue continues. 'The Goddess, she summoned the chieftains of the twelve tribes together. She had a gift for all of them, she said, so they all gathered at the standing stones called Moon Henge and had a big feast and stuff.

'Then the Goddess appears, and she has twelve magic items, one for each tribe. They all have amazing powers, but they all have a weakness too, because she wants the chieftains to use them wisely and not go all crazy about it.

'They're all different as well. A dagger for Munbury that can cut through anything except iron, a sickle for Redwater that can sense poison, and a helmet for Sandywell that makes the wearer invincible.'

Rue blinks at the bard a few times, wondering how to finish. Telling stories to an audience isn't as easy as he thought it would be. 'The end?' he says, with a wince.

'Hmm,' says the bard. And, 'Hmm,' again.

'It was bad, wasn't it?'

'Well . . .'

'I'll never be a bard, will I?' Rue looks as though he is about to cry again.

'It wasn't *that* bad,' lies the bard. 'But I'm sure you know a lot more detail you could have added in. Tell me . . . who were the chieftains of the tribes? What were their names?'

Rue's tongue pokes out of his mouth for a moment as he tries to remember. 'Well, there was Ruddle the Healer of Redwater, and Shadow the Hidden of Dark Hollow. Oh, and No-kin the Lost of Munbury, of course. He's my favourite.'

'Tell me about No-kin then. What was he wearing to the feast? What colour was his fur, his eyes? What food did he like to eat? What songs did he sing along with?'

Rue looks at the bard as if he has gone crazy. 'How would I know that? It was thousands of billions of years ago, probably. Everyone who was there is dead now.'

'Ah,' says the bard. 'But you don't need to know what the answers *actually* are. That's where the storytelling comes in. What you told me was not a tale. It was the bones of one: a few facts put in order, without any life breathed into them. What a bard does is to add meat and skin and ears to the bones. Bring the story to life. Make your own No-kin live in your head, and then give him to your audience. Doesn't matter if he's not the same as the real No-kin – like you said: it was thousands of years ago now. Who's still around to tell you you're wrong? A few more years practise and you'll get the hang of it, I'm sure.'

Satisfied that he has put Rue off in the gentlest way possible, and without completely shattering his dreams, the old rabbit begins to get up from the log, ready to head back to the warren for breakfast. He is interrupted by Rue clearing his throat to speak.

'No-kin is a white-furred rabbit, with sky-blue eyes. He has a mane of long hair that he spikes up from his head, like all the warriors of the Ice Waste tribes where he comes from. He wears a dark green tunic and trousers, with a silver torc at his neck. He has a scar down the left-hand side of his face, where an ermine scratched him before he killed it with his bare hands. He eats the same carrots, radishes and turnips as everyone else, but his favourite food is crowberries, which grow on the tundra. He barely speaks, and when he does it is with a strange accent. The other rabbits all want to know why he left his tribe in the Ice Wastes, but he says nothing, and he is the first rabbit to take his gift from the Goddess. It is a copper dagger, as sharp as starlight, which is where its name comes from: Starclaw.'

The bard stares, open-mouthed, at the little rabbit. Rue's eyes have glazed over as he speaks, as if he is seeing something in another world. In a few seconds he has come back to himself, shaking his head to clear it, and looking puzzled, not quite knowing what has happened.

But the bard knows. It was the storyteller's trance: that sideways step into another place, partly in your head, and partly somewhere else. It means that the little rabbit does indeed have a gift, worse luck, and that the bard is the one to do something about it.

As if to confirm it, a cuckoo calls out somewhere in the Thornwood. The first cuckoo of spring, and a sign from the Goddess, if ever there was one.

The bard sighs and mumbles a very rude curse under his breath.

'What's the matter?' Rue asks. 'Did you just say something about badgers' bottoms?'

'What? No. Nothing of the sort,' says the bard. He sighs again. 'Come on, we need to get inside and get this over with.'

'Get what over with?' Rue is more puzzled by the second.

'Asking your father if you can be an apprentice bard, that's what.'

And with a delighted little rabbit skipping along at his heels, the bard heads back to the warren.

CHAPTER TWO

Tunnels

Surprisingly, Chief Hubert is more than happy that little Rue has found a vocation in life. He has six other, older, sons – and they have caused him headache enough.

The eldest, Hubertus, is training to be chieftain one day. His brother, Hubertian, is training too (just in case), and so is the third son, Huberdink. No rabbit could say that Hubert wasn't prepared for anything. Of the next three, Parsley is preparing to leave for the Temple City of Fyr in Thrianta to become a druid, Thyme is learning to be a blacksmith and Dill has finally decided he wants to be a turnip farmer. When it comes to Rue, Hubert has long run out of ideas.

And so it is decided that the bard should take him on his wanderings. The old storyteller has made it clear that he can't personally be his master (although he refuses to say why, exactly) but that he knows just where to take him to find one. They are to leave after the Lupen's Day celebrations that mark the start of spring, with a farewell from the whole warren.

The bard can't help thinking that Hubert will be glad to see the back of him. After all, he has outstayed his welcome by several weeks. It is time and more to be gone, but it will be hard saying goodbye to his brother. As old age creeps ever onward, each farewell stands a good chance of being their last. And with the trouble that the bard has following him ... well, he would count it lucky if old age was the thing that finally sent him to the Land Beyond.

On the morning of Lupen's Day, everyone in the warren dresses in clothes of springtime green and yellow. They wear daffodils and cherry blossom in their hair and in garlands around their necks. They carry staves of fresh-cut hazel with buds of bright new leaves bursting out from the top. Leading wagons full of food and drink up to the standing stones at the edge of the Thornwood, they spend a whole day there: feasting, dancing and singing.

The last of the winter stores are used for the banquet mixed in with the first delicacies of spring. There are clay pots full of jams – blackberry, elderberry, raspberry – platters of acorn bread, dried parsnips, bowls of dandelion leaf salad with toasted pumpkin seeds, fennel cakes, watercress soup, mustard and buttered asparagus.

There are minstrels and stilt walkers, jugglers and acrobats. Children hunt for painted wooden carrots all over the hilltop, and then the Green Rabbit leads them in a dance around the stones (he's really the enormous doorman, covered from head to foot in leaves and branches, and being made to do it as a punishment for falling asleep at his post – but nobody lets on). The bard is called on to tell one last tale: how Lupen was the first rabbit created by the Goddess, and loved so much by her that she was heartbroken when her twin sister Nixha, the goddess of death, came for him with her bow and lethal arrow. So instead of letting him die, the Goddess put his spirit into the moon, where she could look up and see it every night.

His audience applauds, the bard bows, and with that, it is time to leave. Everyone has a hug or a handshake for the bard, and there are many gifts of food for his journey ahead. Rue's mother is crying and his father seems to have something in his eye (definitely not tears, of course). They present him with a good oak walking stave and a travelling cloak lined with wool that will double as a sleeping bag. His little friends give him slaps on the back and tell him how jealous they are of his adventure.

The bard waits until they are all busy, and then walks to the edge of the crowd. His brother, Podkin, is in the thick of things, laughing at the little ones and talking about old times with the other longbeards. He wears a hooded cloak, covering up his false ear, and leans heavily on his staff, but otherwise seems as carried away with springtime excitement as the little kittens. The bard catches his eye and beckons him over for a quiet word. The two share a brief hug, and the bard clasps his brother's shoulders tight.

'You take care of yourself, won't you? I expect to see you again the next time I'm back this way.' His voice shakes a little, as if he is not sure this will be true.

'Don't worry about me,' Podkin says. 'I'm well looked after here, and full of spring spirit. You have your own little apprentice to care for now.' He chuckles to himself. 'I never thought I'd see the day. But I'm happy for you.'

'Toasted turnips,' says the bard, frowning. 'I keep telling you – he's not *my* apprentice. I'm just taking him under my wing until I find someone suitable.'

'Whatever you say, little brother,' Podkin gives a toothless smile.

'I mean it!' the bard says. 'These things have to be done properly. The stories need to be passed on.'

'Will you be passing on more of my story, by any chance?'

'I might. It is a good one, after all.'

Podkin gives his brother a wink as the two step apart. 'Just make sure it's the real story then. Like the one you started last Midwinter. None of that nonsense about beasts and giants and monsters.'

'It will be accurate to the last detail, I can assure you.' The bard bows low, and then the crowd of rabbits sweep him away from his elderly brother, down the hill. Before he knows it, he and Rue are walking along the old Thriantan Road, the echoes of farewells fading behind them.

*

The two walk in companionable silence for a few minutes – staffs striking the earth in time, packs jingling on their backs – before Rue pipes up with his first questions.

'Do you mind if I ask where we're going, sir? And how long it will take to get there? Do you have a master in mind for me? And will you start training me in the meantime – before we reach wherever it is we're heading?'

The bard rolls his eyes. 'I knew it would be like this,' he mutters. 'Can't you just enjoy the lovely spring morning? The sky is blue, the snow is gone. Let's make the most of it, shall we?'

'But, sir, I really should know where we are going.

I'd like to make a map of the route, for when I'm a wandering bard myself.'

'Bards don't make maps. They just remember things.' The bard sighs. 'But if you must know, we are going to the Festival of Clarion. It's a gathering of all the bards from across the Five Realms. Happens every spring. There's bound to be somebody there who'll take you on.'

Rue actually squeals with excitement and starts hopping round and round the bard, almost tripping him up.

'A festival? Of bards? For Clarion, the god of tales and music? Will you be performing? Will *I* be performing? Is it far? Can you teach me a story on the way?'

'By the Goddess's dandelion underpants, do you ever stop asking questions? The festival's at Blackhenge, up on the downs, about a two-day walk from here. If it'll shut you up for five minutes, I *will* tell you a story. But only if you promise to keep quiet!'

Rue presses a finger to his lips for all of ten seconds. Then: 'Can I choose the story? Can I?'

'If you must.'

'Then will you tell what happens next in the story of Podkin? You told us about how he beat the Gorm Lord at Midwinter, but then we never heard the rest.'

'Hmph,' says the bard. 'That's because your friends wanted to hear about fire-breathing badgers and giant rat-ogres instead.'

'But *I* didn't. The Podkin story was a real one, something that was actually true. I would *so* love to hear more. Did he run away from his enemies? Did he stand and fight? How did he become such a hero? Why did they call him the Moonstrider?'

'You're asking questions again!' The bard glares Rue into silence, then adjusts his pack on his shoulders. *It is a real story*, he thinks, *and a good one for the little mite to start his training with*. And besides, hadn't he just promised his brother that he would pass on the tale?

He clears his throat, takes a deep breath and then carries on once more.

*

The bone-faced monster held her blade to Podkin's throat, pushing the jagged edge through his fur and into his skin ...

Oops, no – that's much too far on. How about . . .

Podkin had experienced many emotions in his short life. Happiness, boredom, jealousy, terror – lots and lots of terror – but he didn't think he'd ever been quite as lost and lonely as he was now.

Stop. Hang on a minute.

I'm forgetting that it was a good two months ago that you heard the first part of this story. You've probably forgotten some of it by now, if not everything.

Always start off a sequel with a quick recap. That's lesson number one for you.

So. If I am correct, we left Podkin and his friends running away from their successful raid on the Gorm camp, didn't we?

Do you remember the Gorm? Rabbits from the warren that was once Sandywell, who had dug deep beneath the earth, and uncovered a pillar of living metal that was part of the evil god Gormalech. That thing had once covered all the world with his toxic iron body, right up until the Goddess and her sister tricked him back underground.

Now he had returned, using the Gorm as his

agents. They raided Podkin's warren, forcing him, his big sister Paz and little brother Pook to run for their lives. The Gorm leader, Scramashank himself, was after them: trying to get his paws on the sacred magic dagger of Munbury, named Starclaw.

The little rabbits almost died several times (and Podkin lost his ear, of course), but a kind witch-rabbit named Brigid took them in. She sent them on to a den of vagabonds and runaways known as Boneroot, where they met a blind warrior rabbit called Crom.

His old abandoned warren, Dark Hollow, was where the rabbits ended up hiding, until they stumbled across the Gorm camp and its herd of prisoners.

In a daring raid, they saved their mother, and Podkin himself beat Scramashank by chopping off the Gorm Lord's foot with Starclaw.

That just about covers it, don't you think?

Well. Once all that excitement had passed, the rabbits somehow stumbled their way through the snowy forest of Grimheart, back into its murky depths where Dark Hollow warren was hidden.

The thrill of their success had been huge, Podkin was carried on rabbits' shoulders, spun around and slapped on the back until he was dizzy. But the elation was short lived once the rabbits realised they now had many mouths to feed, and on Midwinter rations too.

There had been scarcely enough food when it was just Crom, the children and Mish and Mash, the acrobatic dwarf rabbits they had saved from Boneroot. There were now fifty more half-starved and wounded escapees to take care of, including Podkin's mother and aunt.

To say that the rest of the winter was difficult would be an enormous understatement. Many of the Gorm's prisoners were too weak or sick to survive on the husks of acorn bread and pine needle soup they were fed. When the snow and ice that cloaked the forest finally began to thaw, there was a new cluster of little gravestones in a clearing near the warren.

Of those that did survive, some chose to move on once they were strong enough. They headed south, down through the forest and into the warmer, safer realms of Orestad and Thrianta. Podkin wished he could follow them but, not even a day after arriving at Dark Hollow, his mother and aunt had both fallen into a deep sleeping sickness. They would wake just enough to take a little water or broth, before sinking back down again. Then, try as they might – with pleas, songs, stories or shouts – Podkin and Paz couldn't get them to respond. Not even a squeeze of a paw or flick of an ear.

There were five other rabbits just as bad, and spooning broth down their throats was all Brigid, Mash and Paz could do to keep them alive. At first Podkin had been terrified, but Brigid had seen the symptoms before.

'It happens sometimes, after a body has been hurt more than it can take,' she told him. 'These poor rabbits have been beaten, starved and left to sleep out in the snow for weeks on end. They're not in the Land Beyond yet, but close – on the path – waiting for their meat and bones to mend. When they're strong enough they'll wake. You'll see.'

Podkin was too scared to ask what would happen if they didn't. Brigid's grim face told him he wouldn't like the answer.

The other surviving rabbits were refugees from all over Gotland and Enderby. Some were from

Munbury and Redwater warrens, but there were also sables from Cherrywood and Ivywick, lops from Applecross, and brindle-furred rabbits from Stormwell and Hillbottom. Some came from tiny warrens Podkin had never heard of, like Toadleton and Muggy Pit. There was even a shield maiden all the way from Blackrock.

Most of them were still too weak to do much except sit by the fire. The longburrow of Dark Hollow had been turned into a kind of hospital, with bedding and blankets covering the floor. Brigid slept there, tending her patients throughout the night and day, with Paz almost constantly by her side, learning about the healing arts as she went. Mash, who knew some herbal lore from his mountain village, helped as well, while Mish led a group of survivors out into the forest every day to forage for food and scout for danger.

Pook spent all his time curled up next to his mother. During the day he sang her made-up songs in his little nonsense language, or quietly played with the scrying bones that Brigid had given him. Podkin was the only one sleeping in the little room they had taken over, and he found it very lonely. Especially at night when he woke, sweating and shouting, from a nightmare – which he did every night, at least once. Terrible dreams of grinding iron and armoured, red-eyed monsters. Of Scramashank, the Gorm Lord, and of his father standing before him with his silver sword, waiting to be cut down.

They were all aware that their enemy would be looking for them. If Scramashank had survived the loss of his foot, then hunting down Podkin would be his first priority. Luckily, they had seen no sign of any Gorm for miles around the warren. So far, at least.

The forest was almost impenetrably thick, with drifts of snow and ice blocking the pathways, but they all knew it was only a matter of time before the Gorm's search would bring them into the forest's heart.

Because of the danger, Crom, Mish and Mash had formed a war council along with Rill, the black-furred shield maiden, Dodge, a grey rabbit from Muggy Pit and Rowan, a tall sable rabbit from Ivywick. They spent most days bunched together in a corner of the longburrow, discussing tactics and whether they should flee south or stay hidden.

Podkin watched these meetings from his spot by the fire, seeing how Crom listened intently to the ideas of the others, nodding or disagreeing in his deep, brusque voice. He had slipped back into the role of a soldier – a captain or general, even – with troops to lead and weakened rabbits to protect. Not so long ago it had just been Podkin and his siblings for Crom to worry about. 'My life and sword are yours to command,' he had said. Now it seemed like Podkin was the least of his worries.

That sounded selfish, and Podkin hated himself for it. But he'd had a taste of being a hero, and now it seemed he was a useless child again. Paz was healing rabbits and caring for their mother – *that* was important. There must be something he could do too?

More than once he had wandered across and sat down at the table, only to find all their talk suddenly drying up, and every pair of eyes staring.

'Yes, Podkin?' Crom would say, somehow always

knowing it was him, even though he couldn't see.

'I was just wondering if we were going to do some training?' Pod would say, or, 'Would anyone care for a cup of nettle tea?'

He could never quite pluck up the courage to tell them that *he* wanted to be included in the council, or at least have some special task or job of his own.

But whatever he said, Crom always replied with a weary, 'Not now, Podkin.' And he was waved away, as if he were just an annoying child, rather than someone who had beaten the Gorm Lord in single combat.

Perhaps Crom was tired from the worry of leading a band of starving refugees. Perhaps he actually *would* have liked to take Podkin out for a bout of training that would inevitably lead to more bruises and a bit of mild concussion. How often had Podkin's father waved him away, just the same, when he'd had warren business to deal with? It didn't make it hurt any less, though.

And that was why he felt so lost.

In truth, he *was* an annoying child, he supposed. There was nothing he could do to change it either.

His magic dagger wasn't needed for anything other than chopping wood, he had no skills because he hadn't listened to a single lesson back in Munbury, and the last time he'd tried to help Brigid he'd only succeeded in spilling half a bowl of soup over his mother's blankets. Paz had tutted at him, and carried on with her perfect spoon-feeding, while Brigid gently shooed him away.

So he sat in his spot by the hearth, watching Crom and the others arguing over tactics, feeling useless and very sorry for himself.

He laid a hand on the copper hilt of Starclaw, where it hung at his side.

Sometimes, when he was angry or scared, he could feel the blade hissing and fizzing with energy – almost as if it were urging him into action. Lately he had been feeling it more and more, as if it were becoming more alive, more powerful. But today it was just cold and lifeless. Even his magic sword couldn't be bothered with him.

Not knowing what to do with himself, and not wanting to be around the others any more, Podkin took a lantern from the wall and headed off into the warren. Perhaps he could discover something interesting in one of the unlit, unexplored chambers. Perhaps it would be something that would help them battle the Gorm, and then he might prove himself useful again.

He headed up a tunnel that he knew led to the old smithy and armoury. He'd been up it once already when they'd all first come to Dark Hollow, looking for supplies and firewood. The warren had once been full of rabbits, with Crom's father as the chieftain, but when Crom had decided not to take over after his father died, they had all packed up and left.

Podkin didn't really understand it himself – something about the warren having a curse, and losing its chief being the final straw. But they must have expected the spell to be broken someday, Podkin thought, as they had stored everything away neatly, leaving stacks of firewood, torches and oil everywhere. He had tried to get the story out of Crom a few times, without any luck so far.

This part of the warren was unlit, and Podkin's lantern cast flickering shadows over the packed earth walls. Here and there a dusty tapestry still hung, showing images of tall, stern, grey-furred rabbits, or pine cones, or even a shadowy horned figure, peering out from the depths of a woven forest. *Hern the Hunter*, thought Podkin, *Lord of Grimheart*. Each warren had a god or goddess they tended to favour. Most followed Estra, the Goddess herself. She was much friendlier and more beautiful and didn't lurk about in shadowy woods, scaring people.

Past the entrance to the smithy was a grand doorway of carved wood, which Podkin knew opened on to a temple to Hern. There was also a library through there, according to Paz, but since Podkin couldn't read, he wasn't really interested. He carried on into the darkness.

Now the burrow got narrower, and the roof lower. There were one or two more doorways – most probably sleeping quarters – and then a steep stairwell, heading down to the next level.

Podkin stopped and stared. Had anybody been down there yet? He didn't think so. The darkness was cold and hungry. It smelt damp and old and empty. Should he go down? Perhaps this sulking business was just silly, and he should head back to the longburrow and make himself useful.

Then the dagger at his hip gave a twitch.

Podkin nearly jumped out of his fur. The lantern in his hand swung, making shadows leap and whirl up the walls. Did Starclaw want him to go down?

It twitched again.

'All right, all right, I'm going,' Podkin said, not liking the way his voice echoed through the chambers below.

He took a deep breath and tiptoed down the stairs.

*

Podkin emerged into a wide chamber, with three doors along the far wall. This part of the warren seemed much older than the level above. His lantern light glinted upon layers of cobwebs, all coated in dust. The earthen walls looked crumbly in places, and here and there a patch of damp had sprouted mushrooms. There were carved pillars around the chamber's edge, worn and splintered. He could make out more pine cones, and some other rabbit figures, but it was as if time had blurred and smudged them. *No one has been down here for years*, he thought. It made him feel a bit guilty, like he was sneaking into someone's secret hideaway.

After a few moments of watching the dust motes swirl in the lantern light, Podkin took a deep breath and stepped into the chamber. His feet crunched on the gritty dust that covered everything, leaving telltale footprints of his presence. Being a rabbit, dark underground rooms didn't normally bother him much, but this was exactly the kind of place you would expect to be haunted.

A quick look behind these doors, and then back to the longburrow, he told himself, trying as hard as he could not to imagine the restless spirits of long-dead rabbits that might be lying in wait for him.

Two of the doorways looked plain and uninteresting, but the third was surrounded by more ornate carvings, and made of thick oak. Some kind of temple? He lifted the copper ring set into the centre and pushed.

To Podkin's surprise, the door swung inwards quite easily. He stepped through to find another large space, this one dominated by a stone statue of the Goddess, with an altar table before it.

She had been standing watch down here for a very long time. There were empty bowls and plates on the altar: the last offerings of food the Dark Hollow rabbits had made, long ago rotted into dust.

A slow, dripping sound came from somewhere in the temple, and Podkin could smell the damp. The walls behind the statue of the Goddess were badly cracked – crumbling even, in some places.

Podkin was about to leave and try the other doors, when something caught his eye in the shadows behind the altar. A deep black hole in the ground, edged with fresh sodden earth. Had something tunnelled up from below? Podkin remembered the way the Gorm had burst up from beneath and into his warren, and felt a sudden surge of terror squeeze the breath from his lungs. But no, there were no mounds of soil around the hole. The ground had fallen *in*, not been pushed out. This was a collapse of some kind. Damp earth and time had done this, not Gorm.

As he walked forwards to investigate, he felt Starclaw twitch again, and then buzz with pent-up energy. Was there something important down there? Was this where the dagger was leading him?

He reached the altar, making the Goddess's sign as he passed, and then edged towards the hole, not trusting the apparently crumbling floor.

When he was close enough to peer into the hole, he lowered the lantern, sending golden beams down into the chasm. There *was* something down there. It looked like more stairs, heading lower into the earth, with some kind of room beyond. A secret chamber? Was it something Crom knew about?

Starclaw was zinging away like a mad thing now, and Podkin knew he had to go down there. On his own, though? That would be stupid. What if the damp earth gave way and he was buried? Nobody even knew where he was. He'd probably starve to death by the time they noticed he was gone.

He needed help, and there was only one rabbit he could ask. Crom and Brigid were too busy, as were Mish and Mash. Pook was too little, so that only left ... Paz.

As much as he hated the idea, he was going to have to ask his sister for help.

CHAPTER THREE

Shade the Cursed

Paz was tending to a comatose rabbit when Podkin got back to the longburrow. It was one of the Applecross lops – a male, he thought – although it was difficult to tell. The poor creature had great bare patches of skin all over his head where his fur had fallen out. His eyes were gummed shut, and his mouth hung open, wheezing rattling breaths. You could see every bone of his skull, and here and there were half-healed gashes and purple mottled bruises where he had been beaten. Podkin felt very sorry for the creature, but it also made him feel queasy to stand so close. It could easily be him lying there – or Paz, or Pook – if they hadn't found that secret passageway and escaped the warren when the Gorm invaded. It might be him yet, if Scramashank ever got hold of him.

His sister didn't seem affected. She was tenderly dabbing some kind of ointment on her patient's wounds. Beside her was a wooden bowl of broth she had been spoon-feeding him with.

'Hello, Pod,' she said when she saw him. Despite having been awake enough to drink soup, the sick rabbit didn't twitch an eyelid.

'Hello,' Podkin said. 'How's Mother?'

Paz looked over to where their mother lay, tucked in a blanket. She looked a bit better off than the lop Paz was tending to, but still in a very bad way. 'She's still sleeping,' his sister said. 'She's put on a bit of flesh with all the broth, but I don't think she's going to wake soon.'

Podkin glanced over to where Brigid was mixing up medicines at one of the tables by the fireside. He moved closer to Paz, as close to the poorly rabbit as he dared, and whispered even more quietly.

'Listen. I know you're busy but ...' He took a deep breath. 'I really need your help with something.'

'Help? You need *my* help?' Paz was as surprised as him, and in that instant Podkin knew she would refuse anyway. Partly to spite him, but also because she thought her healing work was much more important.

'I'd love to, Podkin, but—'

'Yes, you should help him, dear,' Brigid interrupted. She had somehow moved from the table to the lop's bedside both silently and instantly. 'You'll need to take a lantern with you. And Pook as well.'

Podkin was about to ask the old rabbit how she knew what they needed, but then bit his lip. Brigid was a witch-rabbit, and she knew things about the future. She had been expecting them to turn up in the woods, months and months before they actually stumbled into her. It was best to just nod and go along with what she said.

'I can't—' Paz began.

'Nonsense,' said Brigid. 'I'll be fine here. This is important. Off you go.'

41

'I don't see why we need to take Pook, though,' muttered Paz as she scooped him up from their mother's bed. He snuggled into her, blinking his big eyes at Brigid.

'Because he has the luck of the Goddess,' said Brigid.

Podkin allowed himself a secret smile and trotted back off to the lower warren, picking up an extra lantern on the way.

*

The three rabbits stood at the edge of the hole, peering in. With the light from both lanterns, Podkin could see that there were definitely some stairs leading down. Roughly formed, uneven ones, that looked like they'd been hacked out of the earth in a hurry.

'Maybe there's a whole other warren under this one,' Podkin said. 'Like this level is under the one we've been living in.'

'Could be,' said Paz. 'Dark Hollow is one of the oldest warrens around. Or it could just be an old wine cellar or something.'

'Would Brigid say a wine cellar was important?

Come on, let's go down.' Podkin was still a bit worried about being buried alive, but Brigid's enthusiasm had infected him, and Starclaw was humming quietly at his hip. There *had* to be something important down there. He lowered himself over the edge of the hole and on to the wonky staircase.

'I really think we should go back for some rope or something,' Paz said, passing Pook to Podkin and climbing down after him.

'Stop worrying,' said Podkin. 'Look at this!'

He was at the bottom of the narrow stairs now, and his lantern lit up the top end of a wide, round room. Soil had fallen into most of it, leaving only a small section to stand in – a bite-sized chunk out of a wall of mud and matted roots. You could see it must have been quite a place, though: at least as big as the longburrow above.

'Ooh!' said Pook, staring around with wide eyes.

'The floor!' said Paz.

Looking down, Podkin could see great clods of mud where the roof above had collapsed. In between were hundreds of tiny clay tiles, laid in careful patterns of weaving whorls and pine cone emblems.

Mosaics, he remembered from some distant history lesson back in Munbury. They were beautiful and delicate – almost too special to walk on.

Podkin shone his lantern at the walls beside him. The packed earth had been whitewashed, and then painted with simple figures. They had faded almost to nothing, but he could make out several rabbit shapes, all with horns on their heads. Hern, the hunters' god again, or was that how the ancient Dark Hollowers dressed?

'This place is *really* old,' he said.

Paz nodded. 'There's a door over there.'

They walked over to it, feet crunching on the clods of soil dotted about the floor. It was a wooden door, heavy oak by the look of it, set into a thick frame that was carved all over with weaving branches. From in between the thickets the horned rabbit Hern could be seen again. In the flickering lamplight, it looked as though he gave Podkin a wink. Surely just his imagination playing tricks on him. He touched a finger to the carving to make sure. Yes. The wood was more like lifeless stone, turned black and solid with time. A copper ring in the centre acted as a handle, but instead of a keyhole there was a cluster of raised stones, each marked with a crude symbol.

Podkin tried the door. It was like trying to push a boulder. 'It's locked,' he said.

'You don't say,' said Paz, making him growl. 'Look at those stones, though. Have you seen the pictures before? They look very familiar.'

Pook, still snuggled on Paz's hip, had been busy staring at the horned rabbit carvings. But when he saw the marked stones, he began to wriggle like crazy, squeaking and trying to get at them with his chubby fingers.

'Owns! Owns!'

Paz struggled to hold him and moved back from the door. 'You don't own anything, Pook. Stop wriggling, will you!'

'Not "owns" – he's saying *bones*!' Podkin remembered how Pook loved casting Brigid's set of carved scrying bones, and also how he'd shown almost miraculous luck at playing a dice game when they had been captured by a pair of villainous rabbits in Boneroot.

'Those symbols are the same as the ones on

Brigid's bones, aren't they, Pook? Move him closer to the door, Paz. Let him press them.'

'What, you think that pressing letters is somehow going to open this door?' Paz gave Podkin a scornful look as she shoved Pook up to the door handle. His fingers started tracing the symbols and pushing them here and there, making a series of clicking sounds.

'Just watch,' said Podkin. He folded his arms and gave Paz his best smug smile.

'There's ten stones there, Podkin. There must be millions of different combinations. There's absolutely no way—'

She was interrupted by a loud *clank*, and the door began to swing inwards with a deep grinding sound.

'In we go!' Podkin skipped in front of Paz, immensely enjoying the amazed look on her face.

*

The room inside had partially collapsed, just like the longburrow chamber they had come from. Another bank of earth blocked off all but a small section. Just enough to see that it had once been equally as grand. More mosaic floors, painted figures and hollows in the wall where sculptures or lanterns had once stood.

'What was this place?' Podkin asked.

'Well, if the other room was the longburrow, then this would be the right place for the chieftain's chamber,' said Paz.

A chieftain's room, Podkin thought. That explained why it felt so grand. But what did Starclaw want down here? There was nothing left except a mound of splintered wood, half buried by the fallen earth.

Paz moved closer to it, bringing her lantern down to see better.

'Looks like this was the chieftain's bed, or something,' she said. 'There's a name carved on it. Can you see?'

Podkin shone his lantern on the broken bed too. There *was* something, carved in Ogham, on what might have been the footboard. He couldn't read the patterns of lines that made up the writing, but Paz could.

'What does it say?' he asked.

'A name, I think? Shard, maybe? The wood is all crumbly ... Shade?'

'Was there a chief called Shade here?' The name sounded familiar to Podkin. As if to confirm it, Starclaw zapped his leg with an excited bolt of energy.

'Of course!' Paz slapped a paw to her head. 'Shade the Cursed! There was a scroll about him in the library when Brigid and I were looking for potion recipes She told me it was important that I read it.'

'Sometimes,' said Podkin, 'I think it would be a lot easier if she just *told* us all the things we needed to know in one go, instead of all this mystical hinting nonsense. What did the scroll say?'

'I can't quite remember,' said Paz. 'I only glanced at it really. I should have known it was one of Brigid's clues. I think he brought a curse on Dark Hollow warren. I'm not sure how, only that he doomed them all to bad luck. Probably why they were so keen to be off once Crom refused to be chieftain. Who wants to live in a jinxed warren?'

'Us, apparently.' Podkin drew Starclaw from its sheath and held it up by the broken bed. He could actually *see* the dagger jiggling from side to side in his paws.

'What are you doing?' Paz asked.

'Starclaw is going crazy,' Podkin explained. 'There's something down here it wants me to find.'

'Treasure, do you think?' Podkin had told Paz before how the dagger sometimes moved or buzzed, almost as if it were alive. 'Could it be another one of the Twelve Gifts? Crom always said he didn't know what had happened to Dark Hollow's one.'

'Could be.' Podkin's excitement was matching Starclaw's now. Just imagine if they were the ones to find the missing Gift! He began to move the dagger around the room, noting where the buzzing became stronger. 'Not over here, or here. It seems to be attracted to something near the bed.'

'Bed! Bed!' Pook called, as if he already knew where it was. Podkin brought the dagger tip down towards the mosaic floor at the end of the ruined footboard. The thing practically jumped out of his paws.

'It's down here, I think,' he said. 'But how are we going to dig it up? We didn't bring a spade.'

'Podkin. Your dagger can cut through *anything*, remember?' Paz shook her head at him, and Pook copied her.

'Oh yes,' muttered Podkin, feeling foolish. He plunged Starclaw down into the floor, feeling bad for a moment about ruining the delicate mosaics, and used it to cut a rough circle, which he then levered up with the blade.

He had exposed a small hole, dug into the ground and covered over with the clay that made up the flooring. Inside was a leather pouch, rotted away to nothing. When he reached down to grasp it, it crumbled, revealing a glint of metal.

'What is it?' Paz and Pook were squeaking with excitement behind him. Pod scooped the whole bundle out on to the floor, and brushed away the pouch fragments to reveal a small silver brooch and a clay tablet. Lines of Ogham writing had been pressed into the clay. He passed it on to Paz, and lifted the brooch to examine it more closely.

It was beautifully made. Silver wires looped and knotted together in an intricate circular pattern. There was a long pin on the back, and some kind of white stone in the centre. It looked like a tiny version of the moon.

'In moon's clear sight, in shadows dressed: this

Gift will make you dance your best,' Paz read. 'It must be the Gift of Dark Hollow! This has been lost for centuries, Podkin!'

A lost sacred treasure, found again. A miracle, or the will of the Goddess maybe – but all Podkin could think about was how pleased Crom would be with him. At last.

CHAPTER FOUR

Moonstrider

All the way back to the longburrow, Podkin clutched the brooch in his paw, thinking of the delight on Crom's face when he heard the news, picturing himself being invited to the head seat on the war council every day, the nods and smiles all the new rabbits would give him when they passed him in the warren.

But no sooner had they stepped out of the tunnel, Podkin's visions disappeared in a puff of imaginary smoke.

There was chaos in the burrow, for what seemed

like several reasons. Firstly, Mish and the scavengers were back, and placed on one of the tables was a large pile of dandelion leaves. The first fresh food of spring, and also the first green things anyone had seen for far too long.

'Dandies!' Pook shouted, and Paz whooped as well. It was something to celebrate, but Podkin could see that the rabbits gathered around the council table were far from happy.

Crom and Brigid were there, Mish and Mash too, and any other rabbit that was fit enough to stand. There was lots of shouting and gesturing going on, and it didn't sound like the good kind.

As Podkin and Paz drew closer, they could hear why.

Mish and her scavengers had travelled right to the forest's edge, where they discovered the winter snow had thawed completely, and patches of dandelions had even started sprouting.

They had also discovered, after harvesting as many leaves as they could carry, that the Gorm were about. A squad of three riders patrolled to the west, near to the crater that had once been Boneroot.

They had been tiny spots in the distance, but the bulky iron forms of Gorm warriors were unmistakable, sitting on the backs of the armoured giant rat-beasts they rode into battle.

Mish had ordered everyone back into the forest, covering their tracks as best they could. They had then dashed for the safety of Dark Hollow as fast as their legs would carry them.

'Were you seen?' Crom asked. 'Are you sure you left no signs?'

'No, not seen,' said Mish. 'And I don't think so. I mean, we were in a hurry ... frightened ...'

Podkin was frightened too. The months spent underground in Dark Hollow had begun to convince him he was safe, even though he knew he wasn't really. His nightly nightmares made sure of that. An actual sighting of the Gorm, though ... it brought the real fear of those evil iron monsters back. He could feel his paws begin to shake.

'Extra scouts in the forest! Double the watch!' Crom ordered. 'Every walking rabbit! We keep lookout for the next two days. At the first sign of Gorm, we run.'

'But the sick rabbits . . .' Brigid began.

Crom's stern face became even more grave. 'In the army we would have had stretchers and strong rabbits to move them, but . . .'

'We'll manage,' said Rill, the shield maiden: a short but well-muscled, black-furred rabbit with quick brown eyes. 'We can make stretchers from wood and blankets. There's enough of us to carry the wounded if we need to.'

'I'm not leaving anyone behind,' said Brigid, eyes flashing.

'It might not come to that,' said Mish. 'They might not spot our tracks. They might go in the other direction completely.'

'Let's hope so,' said Crom. He didn't sound convinced. 'But we need to be ready. Pack food and supplies, just in case.'

He sounds like the chieftain he should have been, Podkin thought, still clutching the brooch in his paw. Should he show him the treasure now? Was the time right?

He looked to Paz for advice, but she just shrugged. She would be worrying about her patients, about their mother and aunt. Would they survive being loaded on to stretchers and dragged through the forest?

But what if the treasure was a way to beat the Gorm? Surely Crom would need to know that?

Podkin took a deep breath and walked up to the blind rabbit, setting a paw on his arm. 'Crom? I have something to tell you.'

'Not now, Podkin.' *Not now ... later ... in a moment.* Not what he wanted to hear, but this was *important.* Pod pressed on.

'But I've found something, Crom. A hidden part of the warren! We think it's the chamber of an old chieftain called Shade—'

'Don't mention that name!' Crom's voice was suddenly full of fury, his blank eyes wide and teeth bared. Podkin leapt away with a squeak. He watched, fur bristling, as Crom made a warding sign – paws up to either side of his head like horns – and then the old warrior visibly pulled himself together, taking deep breaths before kneeling at Podkin's level and reaching out a hand for his shoulder.

'I'm sorry I frightened you, Podkin,' he said. 'But in Dark Hollow we don't say the name of ... of *that* chieftain. He brought a terrible curse down on our tribe, and things have been bleak for us ever since. I knew the old warren was down there, somewhere. My ancestors buried it, long ago.'

'But what did he do that was so bad?' Podkin's voice shook a little when he spoke. He had been so sure Crom would welcome the news, not react like *that*.

'We don't like to say ...'

'He lost Moonfyre, the sacred Gift of Dark Hollow,' Brigid interrupted, giving Podkin a wink she knew Crom would not be able to see. 'Or so everyone thought.'

'Thank you, Brigid.' Crom frowned at her over his shoulder. 'I didn't realise you were so knowledgeable about the history of my tribe.'

'Oh, I know lots of things, I do.' Brigid smiled to herself, then walked off to tend to her patients.

'Anyway,' said Crom, standing. 'That's enough talk. We have lots of things to prepare. I'm sure you can find something to keep yourself busy, Podkin.'

Podkin watched as the big rabbit walked away, already starting to bark orders to those heading out into the woods to keep watch. Paz gave him another shrug, and went off herself to help Brigid, struggling to keep Pook away from the dandelion leaves as they passed.

Podkin was left standing in the centre of the longburrow, the brooch still clutched in his hand. *Keep myself busy?* he thought. *I'll make sure I do.*

*

A few hours later, and it was night in the forest above the warren. Most of the rabbits were still out on watch, shivering in the darkness, probably.

Crom was checking over a pile of packs, stacked at the far end of the longburrow. Supplies, water, blankets, weapons and torches. Everything that could be carried had been bundled up, ready for a hasty escape should the Gorm be seen entering the forest.

Brigid and Paz were doing the same with their medicines, while Mash worked with wooden poles and old blankets, trying to make some kind of stretcher.

Podkin hoped the makeshift stretchers would be strong enough. The thought of leaving his mother and aunt after only just finding them again . . . would he have the strength to run off without them? And if not, would he be brave enough to stay by their side, knowing the Gorm would kill him if he did?

He and Paz had promised each other they would drag the stretchers themselves, if it came to it. He prayed to the Goddess that it wouldn't.

Podkin knew he should be helping with something, but he had a task of his own to be getting on with.

He had spent the early evening puzzling over the riddle they'd found alongside the brooch: '*In moon's clear sight, in shadows dressed: this Gift will make you dance your best.*' What could it mean? Obviously, the first part meant the brooch would only work its magic at night. Perhaps hiding in the shadows too? From what he could gather, each of the Twelve Gifts had a catch to them – some condition or flaw that meant they weren't too powerful. Starclaw, for instance, could cut through anything except iron. Very annoying, considering their enemy was covered in the cursed stuff.

But it was night-time now, the warren was full

of shadows, and the brooch didn't seem to be doing anything much. Maybe he had to be outside, where the moon was? And what would happen if he were? *'Dance your best …'* Would it make him prance around like an idiot? It would be a pretty useless gift if it just did that.

There was only one way to find out.

Making sure everyone was busy, Podkin slipped out of the longburrow and up the tunnel to the warren entrance. There was only one rabbit on guard – all the others were out in the woods, keeping watch in pairs. As Podkin reached the doorway, he saw it was Clary, a soldier-rabbit from Munbury.

'Hello, Podkin,' she said. Podkin smiled. It had been so good to see a familiar face among the rescued prisoners, even though she looked like a ghost of her former self. He'd never actually had much to do with her back in their warren, but being around her now made him feel safe. It was like a little piece of his old world was still there, proving it had once been real.

'Evening, Clary. Crom has given me a message for Mish,' Podkin lied. 'Can I go out and find her?'

'Find her?' Clary laughed. 'You'll be lucky. The little tinker will be halfway up a tree somewhere. More squirrel than rabbit, that one. If I were you, I'd stand out in the open and let her find *you*.'

'Thanks, I'll try that.' Podkin felt bad about lying, but there was no way Clary would just allow him out into the forest at night on his own to play around with some musty old jewellery. He let her open the heavy entrance door, then gave her a wave as he stepped through.

'Be careful, Podkin. Don't go too far into the woods and don't be long. There could be anything out there.'

'I won't,' Podkin lied again. Thoughts of Gorm warriors (*Scramashank*!) or horned rabbit-gods creeping through the trees ran through his mind as the door clunked shut. The forest was very dark, very empty and he was all alone.

*

A quick scurry along the path, and Podkin was soon out of sight of the warren. The first thing he did was look up for the moon. At least, he tried to, but the thick pine trees blocked out all but the tiniest specks of sky. He peered at the brooch anyway, and wasn't surprised to find it as cold and lifeless as ever.

He needed a clearing, somewhere the trees weren't so crowded. There was one nearby, but the thought of it made his fur stand up with fear.

The graveyard.

Not a place you wanted to be on your own at night.

Come on, Podkin, he told himself. *You've faced worse things than a dark graveyard.* True, but *that* made him start thinking of Scramashank again, and his fur bristled even more.

This was ridiculous. Did he want to be a scared, tiny rabbit, hiding behind warriors like Crom and Clary? No. He wanted to be a chieftain's son. He wanted to be an important part of the warren, like Paz was. *Fears are there to be faced*, a voice in his head whispered. It sounded like something his father would say, and marching to the graveyard was something his father would have done.

Podkin took a deep breath, gripped Starclaw at his side, and headed through the forest to the clearing.

*

The graveyard was a short walk away, but it seemed much longer at night. The blackened trunks and roots of trees became Gorm warriors, their crooked blades and spears poised to skewer Pod. Branches that brushed his cloak and trousers were clawed metal hands, reaching out to pull him under the earth. By the time he reached the edge of the graveyard he was breathing heavily, and he'd been squeezing the hilt of Starclaw so hard his fingers hurt.

But he got there safely. Funny how something that would have seemed like an adventure months ago – before the Gorm, before losing his father – was now filled with hidden terrors. Was this how it would always be? Would he ever get rid of this constant fear?

Starclaw gave a little buzz at his side, reassuring him. And of course he had the brooch too. Moonfyre, Brigid had called it. Sure signs that the Goddess was protecting him. *There's nothing to be afraid of, Podkin,* he told himself. *Get on with your mission.*

He looked out across the clearing. Twelve little mounds of earth now filled it, each with a tiny wooden headstone. Podkin remembered how they had had to hack holes out of the frozen ground to lay the shrouded bodies inside. How wasted and broken the poor rabbits had looked, but also, in a strange way, how peaceful. For them, at least the worst was over. He said a little prayer to the Goddess, and turned his gaze upwards to the sky.

Between the treetops, a few pale clouds drifted across an open patch of night. Beyond them, stars: Clarion's harp, the vole, the big radish – and there, in the middle, a gibbous moon, shining silver light over everything.

Podkin held out the brooch, letting the moonlight fall on it. It glittered across the metalwork, and the white stone in the middle seemed to drink it in, glowing from inside in reply. Podkin gritted his teeth, in case the thing made him start dancing the Bramble Reel, but nothing happened. *'In shadows dressed'*. He had forgotten that part of the riddle.

Looking around, he spotted a purple-black smudge of shadow at the foot of an ancient pine. He nervously stepped into it with both paws. 'Come on then,' he said to Moonfyre. 'Do your magic. Make me prance about like a drunken ferret if you want, but do *something*.'

Still nothing.

Podkin scratched his head. He was out in the moonlight. He was dressed in shadow. What more did he need? Starclaw just *worked* when you wanted it to, but without knowing what Moonfyre did, how could he use it?

He looked out at the graveyard again. Maybe he needed to be more in the open, away from the treeline. There, by the graves, maybe? Or on the other side, where the sharp black shadows of that lopsided aspen lay?

Then there was a *swish*, a falling sensation, the ground zipping away from his feet. One instant he was standing at the clearing edge, looking at the shadows, the next he was standing beside the aspen, looking back at his footprints.

What had happened? Had he jumped from one side of the graveyard to the other? Or had he somehow moved in between the shadows, disappearing from one place and appearing somewhere else?

He decided to try again.

This time he looked at the soft patch of darkness on the right-hand side of the clearing, where a fallen tree trunk was being slowly swallowed by moss and loam. He imagined himself standing there, moving from *this* place to *that*.

The *swish* came again. He had the same feeling of toppling, and then there was soft squidgy moss between his toes. He was standing by the log.

'*This Gift will make you dance your best . . .*' Not actual dancing, like at Midwinter or Lupen's Day, but dancing in between the shadows cast by the moonlight. He had discovered Moonfyre's power, and he hadn't even had to ask for Paz's help!

Podkin was about to dash back to the longburrow to tell Crom – surely he would want to listen *now* – when he heard voices in the forest. Footsteps too, and they were heading his way.

Without really thinking what he was doing, Podkin flicked his eyes around the graveyard, focusing on the deep shadows of a bramble bush at the far side. In a heartbeat he was there, crouching amongst the thorns, some of them digging into his fur, making him want to squeal.

He held his breath, watching, thinking, *Gorm, Gorm!* But instead two lop rabbits walked into the graveyard. Part of the scout patrols, that was all.

One was the huge blacksmith from Applecross warren. Sorrel, Podkin thought he was called. The other was another Applecross lop. He wasn't sure of her name: Tansy? Pansy? Something like that. They would mean him no harm, but Podkin stayed hidden, taking the quietest breaths he could. After all, how would he explain being out on his own in the graveyard at night? And he still didn't know these rabbits very well. He was wary of all strangers now, after the things that had happened to him since last Midwinter.

But the rabbits were up to more than just patrolling. There was something sneaky – furtive – in the way they were moving. Podkin watched and listened.

'Can we talk here?' Tansy or Pansy was looking round the clearing, checking if they were alone. She clutched at the huge arm of Sorrel, as if she were afraid of something.

'It seems safe.' Sorrel was glancing around

too, but neither of them saw Podkin, buried in the brambles. What were they up to?

'Listen,' said Tansy/Pansy. 'Spring is here. We should leave now, before the Gorm find this place. It's only a matter of time before they search the forest.'

'I've told you before,' Sorrel whispered back. 'I can't take you with me. I promised priestess Comfrey that I wouldn't tell *anyone*.'

'But Sorrel! You can't go back to Applecross on your own! It'll be full of Gorm! Comfrey wouldn't care that you told me – Goddess knows, she's probably dead by now – the most important thing is that we get the hammer back!'

'The hammer is hidden, the Gorm will never find it.' Sorrel growled the words, both a whisper and a shout. 'I've sworn not to tell, and I won't break my vow. When I'm sure it's safe, I'll go back for it. Until then, we stay *away* from Applecross warren!'

Tansy/Pansy was not giving up. 'What about the arrows you made with the hammer? Don't you think these rabbits need to know that there's a way to make weapons that can pierce the Gorm's armour? Just think what they could do with it!'

'And what if we failed to bring it back here? What if the Gorm got their hands on it? I won't let Comfrey's sacrifice be for nothing. There's no way I'm telling you where it's hidden, Tansy. Just forget about it.'

The argument would have gone on, but Podkin heard more footsteps, this time very close to where he was hiding. The tiny form of Mish, the dwarf rabbit, along with another scout, entered the clearing.

'Anything to report?' Mish asked of the two lops. They nearly jumped out of their fur, and looked very sheepish.

'Nothing,' said Sorrel. 'No Gorm this way.' Tansy just shook her head.

'Good,' said Mish. 'You two, go back to the warren for some sleep. Come and relieve us in a few hours.'

Sorrel nodded. He and Tansy left the clearing, heading back to the warren. Podkin waited until Mish and her partner had walked off in the opposite direction before he dared to breathe again.

His head was reeling. The Applecross Gift was hidden away? And it could be used to make weapons that might beat the Gorm?

Just wait until Crom heard about *this*.

CHAPTER FIVE

War Council

This time Podkin didn't even bother speaking to Crom. He walked straight up to where the old warrior was triple-checking the packs of supplies, grabbed hold of his scarred, grey-furred paw and slapped the moon brooch on to it.

'Podkin? Is that you?' Crom asked. 'What's this?'

'*That*,' said Podkin, 'is the lost Gift of Dark Hollow warren. A brooch that lets you jump in and out of moon shadows. I ... I mean *we* ... found it in the hidden warren you didn't want to hear about, and I've just been outside, learning how to use it.'

Podkin stood back, arms folded, beaming, and watched Crom's reaction.

First he frowned, looking as though he was about to shout again. He ran his fingertips over Moonfyre, eyes widening as he realised what it was. Then his face softened. His bottom lip and hands began to tremble. The tall fierce warrior sank to his knees, holding the brooch up as if his blank eyes could see it.

Without a word he reached out a hand towards Podkin's one-eared head. He grabbed the little rabbit and pulled him close against his chest. Podkin could smell the leather of Crom's armour, the linseed oil he'd used to clean it, and underneath, the musky scent of the soldier-rabbit himself. He let himself be held for a few moments before returning the hug, squeezing his protector tight.

'Podkin,' Crom whispered. 'Do you know what you've done? Do you know what this means?'

'Is it good?' Podkin replied, worried that he had upset Crom again.

'Good? *Good?* It's a miracle! You've healed the warren! The curse of Dark Hollow is gone!'

Podkin didn't want the hug to end, but he had more to tell. 'Crom,' he said. 'There's something else you need to know. Something I saw in the forest.'

Now Crom listened. He listened as Podkin told him all about the Applecross rabbits and how he had hidden in the brambles, hearing every word they'd said.

When he had finished, Crom was silent for a few moments. Finally he stood, bellowing across the longburrow in a voice that echoed throughout the entire warren. 'Clary! Rill! Dodge! Get up! Bring me the Applecross rabbits and call the council! Right now!'

*

There seemed to be a lot of running and shouting after that. At some point, Paz came and stood next to him, a sleeping Pook in her arms.

'Podkin, what have you done?' she whispered in his good ear.

'Umm . . . I'm not sure.' Podkin bit his lip. 'Maybe got some rabbits into big trouble?'

Moments later, Sorrel and Tansy were dragged from their room and brought into the longburrow.

Podkin was shocked to see Clary and some of the other soldier-rabbits pointing spears at them.

They were made to stand in front of Crom, who had Rill, Dodge and Rowan – his war council – around him. Brigid was there too, looking a bit less fierce than the others.

'What's this about?' asked Sorrel. His chest was puffed out, his huge biceps tense, as if he were ready to fight. Podkin could see the burn marks in the fur of his hands, face and ears from his work as a blacksmith. He looked as if he'd be just as good at pounding heads as he was copper and bronze.

'You've been keeping something from us,' said Crom. His voice was flat and even, but the frown on his face showed he meant business. Podkin hoped Sorrel wouldn't underestimate him. Even though he was blind, Crom was still one of the best fighters in the Five Realms.

'Keeping something? I don't know what you mean.'

'You were heard,' said Crom. 'Talking about the hammer of Applecross. You know where it is. And what it can do.'

'Heard? By who?' Sorrel looked around the room, eyes flashing. Podkin tried to edge behind Paz without being noticed.

'By Podkin.' Crom pointed a finger at Pod, ruining his hiding plan. He let out a little squeak.

'That one-eared kitten? He's making up stories.'

'You're going to tell us eventually,' said Brigid. 'So you may as well get on with it.'

To Podkin's surprise, Tansy nudged him on. 'Go on, Sorrel,' she said. 'There's no point hiding it any more.'

Here it comes, Podkin thought. *He's going to go crazy, and I'm going to get squished like a beetroot.* But instead of flying into a rage, the smith's huge shoulders sagged. He let out a deep sigh, sounding almost relieved.

'Very well,' Sorrel said. 'I suppose there's no point in keeping quiet. Although I would like it noted that I kept my vow. The secret was found out before I spoke.'

'Noted,' said Crom and Brigid together.

The soldier-rabbits lowered their spears, and Rowan fetched a chair for Sorrel. Once he was seated, he began to talk.

'For any that don't know, I am from Applecross warren. I am – I *was* – the master smith there. We were famous throughout all Gotland, you know, for our metalwork. Blessed by the Goddess, we thought, and especially because of our Gift: the sacred hammer, Surestrike.

'We didn't use it often, because every time you created something with it, the hammer got slightly smaller. It gave a bit of itself to whatever it made, we used to say. But we were so proud of it, anyway, and Chief Brae had it displayed on the wall over the longburrow hearth.

'Anyway. The Gorm came. We heard stories from the north of Enderby. Warrens being taken over, rabbits being dragged off . . . We didn't believe it at first, or we thought it was too far away to bother us.

'Then we started to get survivors coming to our warren. Rabbits from Stormwell and Hillbottom. That was when we knew the stories were true. The Gorm were real, and they were coming our way.

'Chief Brae started to get the warren ready. We made more armour, more weapons. One day he asked me to take the sacred hammer down. He told me to make some arrowheads with it. Small ones, that wouldn't use up too much of the hammer's essence.

'I was very honoured. I'd seen my father use Surestrike once, but it was the first time I'd been allowed to touch it. I made five bronze arrowheads with it, and they were the finest things I'd ever crafted. They just seemed to flow out of the metal: perfect they were, and they shimmered like some unseen light was shining on them . . .

'Well. We fitted them to arrow shafts and we waited. Sure enough, the Gorm did come. Scramashank himself, pretending to talk truce, and then his warriors tunnelled up from the ground, right into our longburrow.'

Podkin shivered at this point, and cuddled in close to Paz. That was exactly what had happened to their own warren, not long ago.

'There was a lot of fighting. A lot of screaming and shouting. It was hard to see what went on . . .

'I *did* see Chief Brae fire those arrows, though. Five shots, and each one tore through that Gorm armour like it was wet lettuce. Five Gorm fell down dead, but they were the only ones. All our other weapons just bounced off the monsters.

'That was when Brae knew it was over. He tore Surestrike off the wall and gave it to Comfrey, our priestess. She grabbed me and together we ran, through a secret tunnel in the fireplace and out of the warren. Others were running too, but the chief stayed until the end. He stayed to make sure we'd escape with the hammer . . .'

Sorrel's voice faltered, and he laid his head in his burn-scarred hands. Tansy moved to stand beside him, and placed a reassuring paw on his shoulders. After a few moments of quiet sobbing he managed to continue.

'Comfrey ran with me. It was dark, but she knew where she was going. There were Gorm outside the warren too, but we dodged them. Applecross is by a lake – she led us down to the water's edge and we ran along it until we were standing across from the island. Ancients' Island, they call it.

'She did something then, I couldn't see what. A bridge appeared, from the shore to the island. I'd lived all my life by that lake, and I never knew a bridge existed, hidden or not.

'Comfrey told me to wait, to guard the bridge, and then she ran across with Surestrike. There are ruins on the island: a tomb, an old, old stone thing. Older than time. I can only guess she hid the hammer there, because when she came back, it was gone.

'She closed the bridge, or hid it again. I don't know – one minute it was there, and the next it wasn't. "Don't tell anyone about this," she said to me. "Swear it by the Goddess." I promised, and then we ran again.

'We didn't get very far. There were Gorm everywhere. I tried to fight them, but it was like punching an anvil. They knocked me down, hurt me bad. Then they hauled me off along with some others. Took me to that camp you found us in.

'As for Comfrey, the last I saw they were dragging her back to Applecross. They knew she was a priestess, I expect. They must have wanted her to give them Surestrike. Either that or to make her one of them. Who knows how those monsters think?'

Sorrel jumped to his feet suddenly, punching

one meaty fist into his other hand. 'If only I'd been stronger! If only I could have fought them off—'

Crom stopped him with a gesture. 'You have nothing to be ashamed of. We've all been beaten by them, at some time or another. This thing you have told us – it could help make a difference. I think you escaped for a reason.'

'You'll go back for the hammer then? Even though the place is full of Gorm? Are you mad?'

'I don't know what we'll do,' said Crom. 'But we all need some time to think. Let's get some sleep, and we can plan in the morning.'

I hope I'll be included, thought Podkin, crossing his fingers as the rabbits all wandered off to their burrows around him. He was the last to go, and was very surprised when Crom knelt beside him.

'Podkin,' he said. 'I think you should have this.' He reached out and pinned Moonfyre on to the little rabbit's jerkin.

'I can't . . .' Podkin began to say, but Crom held up a hand to stop him.

'It chose you,' he said. 'And besides, I have no right to it. I gave up my place as chieftain here a long

81

time ago. It's enough that the Gift has been found again. It gives me hope that one day, with the right chief, this warren might be whole again.'

Crom walked off, smiling to himself, leaving Podkin alone in the longburrow holding not one, but two of the Twelve Gifts. His brain was whirling with all that had happened in one evening. It was too much for a little rabbit's head to take in.

Maybe that was why he saw, or thought he saw, his dagger and the brooch twinkle at each other before he headed off to his room to sleep.

*

Podkin was indeed included in the meeting the next morning, but so was every other rabbit in the warren. It didn't stop him feeling pleased with himself, though. After all, this was all down to him finding the brooch and hearing the Applecross rabbits.

They all stood in a rough circle, ears pricked and arms folded, as Crom explained the situation.

'You've probably heard by now,' he began, 'that we've come across some new information that might help us in our fight against the Gorm.' There was a quiet murmur amongst the rabbits, but nobody looked very surprised. Word travels fast in a small warren, Podkin remembered.

'We've discovered that one of the Twelve Gifts – the hammer of Applecross, to be precise – is hidden away in the ruins on Ancients' Island, at Mirrormoon lake. Sorrel here knows where the tomb is, although not quite how to get into it.'

All eyes turned to the big blacksmith, who flicked his ears and kept his eyes fixed on the longburrow floor.

'We could leave it there, safe in the knowledge that the Gorm will never find it. That would be fine, except for something else we've discovered: Sorrel can use the hammer to make arrowheads that will *pierce Gorm armour.*'

This bit of information clearly *wasn't* well known. There was a gasp of shock, and then a babble of voices all talking at once. Crom let it continue for a few minutes, then raised his hands for silence. When it was quiet enough, Sorrel spoke first.

'It's true. I know where Surestrike is, but to find out exactly where it is hidden and how to open the tomb you would have to speak to Comfrey, our priestess. The last time I saw her, she was being dragged back into Applecross warren by the Gorm. She wasn't at the camp with the rest of us, so I guess she's still there. Either that, or she's dead.'

'What would they be doing with her?' Mish was standing at the front, not far from Podkin. 'Why wasn't she at the camp?'

'Our guess is they have been torturing her,' answered Crom. 'They want the hammer, just like they wanted the dagger from Munbury. Either they'll be using pain to make her speak, or turning her into a Gorm with one of their metal pillars.'

'But that was two months ago,' said Mish. 'How long can a rabbit withstand either of those things?'

'She was strong,' said Sorrel, his voice quiet and sad. 'Much stronger than me. She'd die before she told them anything, I know it.'

'So if we *were* to try and find the hammer, we would first have to get inside a Gorm-infested warren, find this priestess – if she's even still alive – and get directions to where it's hidden?' Rill shook her head in disbelief. 'It's madness. A total suicide mission.'

Mash was standing on a table so he could see over everyone's shoulders. He was jiggling up and down with excitement. 'But if we *did* get the hammer,' he said, 'we could make arrows that would kill Gorm. We could forge thousands of them. We could wipe out the whole Gorm army!'

'Surestrike can't make that many,' said Sorrel. 'Every time you use it, a little bit of it wears away. I could make hundreds, maybe, if we dared to use it up. Or spears instead. Swords. Daggers . . .'

There was more excited chatter between the rabbits. Gorm-killing swords? What about axes? Could they all have one? Crom raised his hands again.

'This is an important day,' he said, using his general's voice. 'We have to choose our course, and choose it carefully. Do we hide here from the Gorm for as long as we can? Do we run south like the other rabbits, and hope they don't follow? Or do we use this chance to take the fight to them? What is our future going to be?'

'Fight!' yelled the piebald rabbit next to Podkin, and many others joined in, including Mash and Clary. Some were silent, others looked around with scared eyes. Podkin stared up at Paz who frowned, flicking her eyes back to where their sickly mother lay. What was the best thing to do? Every instinct he had told him to run, just as it always did in the face of danger. He was a rabbit, after all. Running was what kept them alive. But he'd overcome that instinct before, and when he did it usually led to surprising victories.

'Fight!' Podkin yelled, not realising that everyone else had finished shouting. His little voice rang out across the longburrow, drawing stares from all around. Under his fur, he blushed crimson.

'I'm glad Podkin feels the same as I do,' said Crom. Several rabbits chuckled. 'This is a chance we can't miss. What do you say, Brigid? You always seem to know what we're going to do anyway . . .'

Brigid took a long look round the circle of rabbits, her twinkling eyes coming to rest on Podkin. 'They say the best form of defence is to attack,' she said. 'And the Gorm won't be expecting an attack from a little slip of a rabbit like Podkin. He should lead the mission, although he will need some help, of course.'

'Lead? Mission?' Podkin whispered. He hadn't

been volunteering for anything, just joining in with the moment! What was Brigid talking about?

Some of the other rabbits were as surprised as him. Most of them had been too sick or confused to see what had happened when Podkin fought Scramashank at the camp they were imprisoned in. The idea of a child rabbit going on such a quest was a joke to them.

'What's that mad old crone talking about?' Sorrel shouted. 'If we *are* going back, then I should be the one to lead. I was there when Surestrike was hidden, remember?'

'Can anyone use the hammer?' a young voice came from behind Podkin. It took him a moment to realise that it was Paz.

Sorrel blinked for a few moments, then shrugged. 'I was shown how to use it when I became master smith. There's a special knack to it, special words to speak – it works differently to any other hammer. But I could train someone else, I suppose. If they were skilled enough.'

Paz made a show of looking around the rag-tag bunch of rabbits in the longburrow. 'But we don't have anyone skilled enough, do we? We don't have anyone who knows the first thing about smithing. If we lose you to the Gorm, then the hammer is useless, even if we do manage to find it.'

'An excellent point, from a clever young lady,' said Brigid. 'Such intelligence will be needed on the mission as well.'

'You are joking, aren't you?' Sorrel couldn't believe what he was hearing. 'Someone tell me she's joking? The next thing you know, she'll be saying the little baby has to go as well!'

Crom sighed. He already had experience of Brigid and her knowledge of the future. 'You're going to tell us to take Pook, aren't you?'

Brigid shook her head. 'He's but a baby, although it will be hard for him to be parted from his brother and sister, especially with his mother still sick. No, he will stay here and I shall care for him. The other two must go, however. This thing has been foreseen, and the children must be there, otherwise the hammer will be lost. I can't tell you much else, except that there *will* be time to speak to the priestess if you hurry. My senses tell me she is still alive and still herself. Her connection to the Goddess was strong, and will last a little time yet. But you must be quick, and you must take Pod and Paz. Who else goes is up to you.'

'You're all as crazy as a nest of weasels!' Sorrel yelled. 'Well, you can suit yourselves. Charge into Applecross riding a shaved badger if you like. You're all going to end up dead. I'll wait here for two weeks, just in case there's a miracle and you *do* bring back the hammer. After that, I'm heading south to Thrianta. The rabbits there can't be as mad as you lot.'

The blacksmith stomped out of the longburrow, shaking his head. But Podkin was too dazed to notice he'd gone. Had Brigid just said they were going into Gorm territory? To find a lost hammer on a mystical island? He yanked the fur on his arm to see if this was some kind of a nightmare he was stuck in. He'd wanted to be part of things, but not an insanely dangerous mission of doom.

'Oh, Pod, what have we done?' Paz whispered in his ear. There was a flurry of shouting and gesturing all around the room: rabbits asking to go, rabbits saying the idea was stupid, and in between them all, looking at Podkin with a knowing glint in her eye, was Brigid the witch-rabbit.

Not again, thought Podkin, remembering once more the horror of the Gorm: fleeing them, dodging them, fighting them.

Not again. Not again.

INTERLUDE

'This looks like a good spot,' says the bard, breaking off the story.

They have walked all day, along a worn track weaving its way across the top of the Razorback downs. After following it down a slope, they have come to a sheltered little valley full of hawthorn trees, all bursting into fresh leaf.

'A spot for what?' Rue asks. 'What about the story?'

'Plenty of time for that in a bit,' says the bard. 'We're camping here for the night. Can't you see the sun going down?'

Lost in the tale about Podkin, Rue hasn't noticed

the sky beginning to blush pink. In an hour or so it will be dark.

'But I have lots of questions! Important questions!'

'Don't you always,' says the bard. He drops his pack to the floor under one of the hawthorn trees and begins to take off his cloak. 'Can't they wait until dinner's cooked?'

'No, they can't! For example: why do Podkin and Paz have to go on the mission? They've only just escaped Scramashank and the Gorm. Podkin's obviously terrified. Why does the Goddess want to put them in danger again?'

The bard puts his paws on his hips and stares down at his new apprentice with his sternest glare. 'Who are you to know why the Goddess does things? Hasn't it been clear from the start that Podkin is doing her will? He's the bearer of *two* of her Gifts now. Don't you remember all the battles Podkin and Paz have won already? Of course she would choose them.'

'But poor Podkin . . .'

The bard sighs and ruffles Rue's ears. 'I'm glad you're worried about Pod,' he says. 'It shows I'm telling my story well. But look out there.' He points away from the downs to the land beyond. A vast, open plain of green with no trees, hills or buildings in sight. 'That there is the Sea of Grass. Not just ordinary grass, you know, but long stuff that grows taller than your ears.

'There are rabbits that live out there. They make big wheeled craft: kind of wagon carts crossed with sailing ships. Like boats in the grass, they are. And they build warrens on stilts, higher than the treetops.

'They never touch the ground. Do you know why?' Rue shakes his head. 'Because there's snakes out there too. Adders with bodies as thick as oak trunks that could swallow you whole. Sometimes they slither on to the ships and eat everyone aboard. Sometimes they even go into the treetop warrens and bite rabbits with their poison fangs.'

Rue gulps. 'What has this got to do with Podkin?' he says.

'Do you know what age those grass rabbits start driving the sailcarts? Before they can walk, that's when. I've seen them zipping around, racing about like lunatics, giant snakes be damned. At first, though, they're terrified. Screaming, wailing, "don't-make-me-go-on-that-cart-mummy" terrified. Anyone in their right mind would be.'

'How do they learn to drive then? If they're so scared?'

'They face their fears, little one. And bit by bit, they master them. It doesn't mean they get any less scared of snakes – snakes are flipping horrifying – but they can get on with their sailing and put their worries somewhere they won't bother them. And that's what Podkin has to do in order to beat the Gorm. He doesn't think he can do it, not right now, but the Goddess *knows* he can. How do you think he becomes a hero, after all?'

Rue stands silent for a while, staring out at the rippling grass. 'Well, I don't think it's fair,' he says. 'If *I* were the Goddess, I'd choose someone older to do my tasks. Picking on little rabbits is mean.'

The bard is very tempted to tell the little brat that he is really Pook, that he *was actually there* and that being picked on didn't do him any harm.

But that is a secret for another time. Instead

he gives Rue a clonk on the head with his staff. 'Lesson number two, little bard-to-be. It's *my* story and I don't care what you think. Now, get the fire lit and cook up some soup. I'll carry on the tale while you're working.'

CHAPTER SIX

Surprise

The rest of the day saw lots of hectic planning and preparation for the mission ahead. This included both of the little rabbits, no matter how scared Podkin was about facing the Gorm again.

Pook knew something was up, and he wasn't happy. Even though nobody had said anything to him, he had worked out that Podkin and Paz were going somewhere, and so spent most of his time clinging to one of them, or following them around like a chubby little shadow.

As for the rest of the expedition party, it had

been decided that Crom should definitely go along, and Tansy too. After all, she knew Applecross and how to sneak into it. Mish and Mash both wanted to go, but Mish was needed at the warren to run the council and the scouting parties. The twin rabbits were very upset to be leaving each other, but Mash could hardly contain his excitement at having something to do other than spooning soup into sick rabbits.

Several others wanted to come as well, but eventually they agreed that it was best to keep the group as small as possible. There was less chance of being spotted by the Gorm that way.

Podkin wanted to make the group even smaller. He made a point of catching Brigid on her own one morning, when the others were counting out supplies. He crept up behind her and tugged on her cloak.

'Hello, Podkin,' she said, and then sighed. She obviously knew this difficult conversation had been coming.

Podkin knew she knew, and probably she also knew how it would finish, which made the whole thing very tricky. He wasn't sure whether to start at the beginning, end or middle.

'Look,' he said. 'Are you sure that—'

'Yes, I am.'

'And there's no other—'

'No, there isn't.'

'But I don't—'

'Understand?' Brigid put a hand on his shoulder and lowered her head until it was almost touching his. 'Nobody understands, Podkin. Least of all me. I know it's crazy to be sending you and Paz. I know what terrible things could happen to you both, and that it would be my fault if they did. But every art I have says the same thing, my dear: the bones, the cards, the tea leaves – my dreams, even. They all show me that the hammer will be lost unless you go to find it. I've known this since before I met you. Since before you were born.'

Podkin felt his stomach churning. He'd known she was going to say something like this, but a small part of him had hoped she would change her mind. 'Can you see whether we'll be safe?' he asked. Brigid shook her head.

'I'm sorry, Podkin dear. I don't know if either of you will come back, or even if you'll find the hammer. All I know is what will happen if you don't try. It will be the end for all of us, that's for certain. When you look at it like that, sending you out there is actually safer than keeping you here, as dangerous as it might seem. Do you see?'

'I see,' said Podkin, although he really didn't.

Brigid had a way of looking so deeply into your eyes, it seemed as though she was reading the contents of your brain. 'You want to be an important rabbit, don't you, Podkin?' He nodded. 'A great rabbit like your father? A vital part of our warren here?'

'Yes,' he said. 'More than anything.'

'Well, you're already well on your way. Your father would be so proud of the things you've done. And I know this task we are asking is hard. I know everything that has happened to you before is telling your brain to run *away* from the Gorm, not towards them.'

Podkin gulped.

'I didn't know your father, but I know what he would have been feeling every time he had to make

101

a hard decision or stand up to fight for something. He would have felt scared, just like you do now. But he did those things anyway, didn't he?'

Podkin thought of his father, standing up to Scramashank on the night the Gorm invaded his warren. He realised that, until now, he hadn't imagined how his father would have felt, knowing that he probably wasn't going to survive. It made him feel a bit ashamed for being so cowardly.

Brigid continued. 'You're not being cowardly, Podkin.' (*How did she do that?*) 'You're just feeling the same way any little rabbit would. Goddess knows, after the things you've been through ... If you really don't want to find the hammer, we'll all understand. But if you do, then you would be helping all of us. Me, Crom, your mother and aunt. All of the Five Realms.'

When she put it like that, how could he refuse? *Be like your father*, he told himself. *Put your fears aside*. He gave Brigid a hug and then went to help Paz pack their bags.

'What were you talking to Brigid about?' his sister asked him.

'Going on this mission,' he said. 'I've got a feeling the old witch just played me like a bard plays a harp.'

'Don't worry,' Paz whispered. 'I think we'll be safe. Look what Brigid gave me to help us.'

She opened a fold of her tunic to show him Brigid's magic sickle. The witch-rabbit had entrusted Paz with the sacred Gift of Redwater warren. Podkin's eyes went wide.

'She let you have *that*?'

'I'm just borrowing it,' said Paz. 'Brigid said I was supposed to have it. She even told me its true name – Ailfew.'

Suddenly, Podkin remembered the brooch. In all the excitement, he had forgotten to tell Paz about it. He could do better than telling her, though ... it was dusk now – the moon might be up outside the warren.

'Come with me,' he said, grabbing Paz's paw.

'What? Where? We're supposed to be packing our supplies!' Despite moaning, Paz allowed herself to be dragged across the longburrow, towards the entrance tunnel.

'I've got something to show you,' said Podkin, grinning. 'Something *amazing*.'

They were just heading down the tunnel when Brigid stopped them. Podkin thought she was going to tell them to carry on packing, but instead she handed him a dusty old scroll. 'Get your sister to read this to you,' she said, with one of her knowing smiles. Podkin now knew a mysterious clue when he saw one. He took the scroll and rolled his eyes.

'Thanks, Brigid,' he said. The two little rabbits ran past the old healer and out through the tunnel, into the forest beyond.

*

Podkin was pleased to see that the moon was indeed out. He dashed through the trees with Paz close behind, zigging and zagging through the gathering shadows until he reached the graveyard clearing and the puddle of shadow at the foot of the old aspen.

'This had better be good, Pod,' said Paz when she caught up with him. She was out of breath, but clearly intrigued by how excited her little brother was.

'Look at me,' said Podkin, checking to see the moon was still visible in the patch of sky above. 'Look at me *very closely.*'

'Do I have to?' Paz answered, and was about to

stick her tongue out at him when Podkin vanished. A small rush of air and he was gone.

'Pod?' Paz waved a paw through the space where he had been a second ago. 'Podkin! Where are you?'

'Over here!' Podkin was watching her from the bramble bush he had hidden in before. The shadows were so deep, Paz had no idea he was there. He couldn't help but giggle.

'This isn't funny, Podkin! Where in the Goddess's name are you?'

Now Podkin focused on the shadow Paz was casting herself. He felt the tingling power of Moonfyre, willed himself to be there and ... *swish*!

'Whiskers!' Paz screamed and jumped clear off the ground as Podkin blinked into existence right beside her. It was so funny, he fell on the ground laughing and couldn't get up for a good five minutes.

Paz stood watching him, hands on her hips. 'Have you quite finished? It wasn't *that* funny.'

'Oh, it definitely was,' said Podkin, getting up and brushing the pine needles from his jerkin.

'Was that the moon brooch?' Paz asked. 'Is that its power?'

'It is,' said Podkin. 'You can jump from shadow to shadow, as long as the moon's out. That's how I heard Sorrel and Tansy last night.'

Paz stared at him, wide-eyed. 'You were right,' she said. 'It *is* amazing.'

A sudden thought came to Podkin. Would he be able to jump along with someone else? It was worth a try, he supposed.

'Give me your paw.'

'Why?' Paz's ears twitched and she edged away.

'I want to see if you can jump with me. Don't worry, it doesn't hurt or anything.'

'I don't think we sh—' Paz began, but Podkin snatched hold of her arm before she could finish and aimed his mind at the bramble bush again. There was the familiar lurch – a bit stronger this time – and then he was inside the cave of branches and thorns once more, Paz crouching beside him.

'Podkin!' She punched him on the arm. 'You ferret-face! I was about to say it might not be safe! We could have ended up in the middle of a tree trunk or something!'

Podkin rubbed his arm and scowled at her. 'We

didn't though, did we? Besides, I don't think it lets you jump *into* anything. See how the brambles are all pushed out of our way?'

'Not quite,' said Paz, squirming away from the thorns that were jabbing her bottom. But she did see what Podkin meant. Their bodies had pushed all the roots and brambles aside; otherwise they would have been threaded through with them.

'It's good though, isn't it?' Podkin said. 'Just think of the things we can do with *this*.'

'As long as the moon's out,' Paz reminded him. They sat in their little cave of thorns and looked at the dark forest. Where it had seemed creepy the night before, Podkin now felt peaceful and at home. Maybe because he knew he had to leave and there was a good chance he may never come back.

They watched together as the trees slowly vanished in darkness, how the shadows spread out from beneath the trunks to merge and meld, like blots of ink on wet paper.

'Have you got that scroll Brigid gave you?' Paz asked, breaking the silence. Podkin handed it to her, and she unravelled it, holding it so a ray of moonlight shone through the thorns and on to the crumbling parchment.

'What does it say?'

'It's that scroll about Shade the Cursed that Brigid told me to read before,' said Paz. 'She must have known I didn't look at it properly.'

'She knows blooming *everything*,' said Podkin. He nudged Paz gently in the ribs, urging her to read.

'"Many moons ago a rabbit called Shade became the chieftain of Dark Hollow",' Paz began. '"The warren there was ancient, one of the first Twelve, and had been granted a Gift by the Goddess: a brooch that let the wearer dance through the moonlight.

'"The Dark Hollow rabbits were children of the Goddess, but they also loved the forest and its lord: Hern the Hunter. Like him, they took great pride in their hunting skills, and would bring down fierce creatures such as wolves and bears as tests of their ability.

'"In Shade's time, the young rabbits of the warren had become more and more fanatic about their hunting. They had begun to live only for the thrill of killing the biggest and most savage prey. They had forgotten the ways of rabbits, and how we always try to live in balance with the world around us.

"'As a result, they were destroying the wildlife of the forest. Whole packs of wolves had been wiped out, whole families of bears destroyed. Shade was horrified, and warned his tribesmen about what they were doing, begging them to stop and change their ways.

"'They didn't listen. The young bucks and does would head out hunting every day, even when there were rooms full of skins for tanning and sewing, and the whole floor of the longburrow was covered in furs. No matter what Shade threatened them with, they wouldn't stop. Perhaps they couldn't.

"'Finally, Shade was forced to commit a terrible act. He knew how proud the Dark Hollow rabbits were of their history – that they were one of the first tribes. One day he called them all to the longburrow and told them what he had done.

"'Because he believed they were no longer fit for the Goddess's blessing, he had taken Moonfyre, the tribe's Gift, and cast it into the deepest part of the forest, where it would never be found. The tribe was no longer blessed, instead it was shamed, matching the actions of its children.

'"The Dark Hollow rabbits were furious. They planned to strip Shade of his chieftainship, to cast him out or even kill him. But when they looked for him the next day, he was nowhere to be found. He had left behind his crown and sword and disappeared into the forest."'

Podkin stared at the brooch in his hand. 'Except he didn't really cast it away, did he? He buried it in his room, for us to find all those years later.'

'It would seem so,' said Paz.

'Do you think he was told to do it?' Podkin asked. 'Like it was all some kind of plan?'

'You mean so that we could find it now?' Paz flicked her ears. 'Who knows, Podkin. You'll have to ask Brigid that one.'

'Does it say what happened to Shade? After he left, I mean?'

Paz shook her head. 'That's it. The brooch was lost, and now it's found.'

'"The curse is broken",' Podkin turned Moonfyre over and over in his paw. 'That's what Crom said.'

'Good. Who wants to live in a cursed warren?' Paz tugged at Podkin's cloak. 'Come on. We'd better get back. It'll be time to leave soon.'

A part of Podkin was tempted to stay in the bramble den, hiding away from the Gorm-filled world outside. But he knew he couldn't. *I hope the Goddess does have a plan*, he thought, getting ready to jump back into the clearing with Paz. *And I hope it's a good one.*

*

They left later that evening, as soon as it was fully dark. Somebody remembered it was Lupen's Day, and the official start of spring. There were no feasts or games, or even a Green Rabbit to chase, like there had been at Munbury in the old, happy days. Just a simple dinner of dandelion leaf salad and acorn bread, and a sad farewell from the rabbits they were leaving behind.

Mish had tears in her eyes, so did Brigid. Pook was nowhere to be found, even though they searched the whole warren. Paz assumed he had gone off in a sulk, and Brigid promised she would find him. Podkin wanted to at least say goodbye to him, but

Crom was insisting they leave now, in order to get as far as they could before daybreak. They gave the longburrow a quick search, but didn't have time for anything else. It made it all the harder to walk out of the door and into the unknown.

Finally, they waved goodbye and headed out into the forest. They were dressed in leather armour, with cloaks and packs all dyed black, so they would blend into the darkness. The plan was to travel at night, and camp during the day, in the hope of avoiding being seen. Podkin remembered all too well the Gorm's crow servants: evil, iron-warped flapping things that spied for their masters. Hopefully they couldn't see in the dark.

It was pitch black as they marched north through the forest. Crom led the way, his fingers seeking out the markings Mish and her scouts had carved into the tree trunks. Without him to guide them they would have been lost within moments, but to Crom the forest was no different, night or day. He took them out amongst the network of narrow paths, further away from Dark Hollow than they had been in months. The other times Podkin had travelled this way, there had been snow shrouding branches and laying in thick marshmallow drifts up against the trees. It had given the place a ghostly glow, softened everything into curves of white and silver.

Now the snow had gone, and the woods were all shades of night – jagged trunks and twisting roots. They walked through pines and spruces at first: trunks crowded together, low branches of scratchy needles that brushed at their ears and faces. It was impossible to see much of the path. They tripped and stumbled their way, kicking up clods of spongy earth and fallen pine cones. The sharp, fresh smell of pine sap filled Podkin's nose. It was a good, clean smell, and he might have actually enjoyed this strange night-time stroll, if it wasn't for his imagination creating shapes of Gorm soldiers hiding behind every trunk.

They walked in silence, the only sounds were their breathing and the occasional clink of metal buckles as their packs bounced on their backs. Crom and Tansy used their spears as walking staves, while Mash skipped between the trees as if he could see in the dark. Podkin stayed close to Paz, one hand on

Starclaw's hilt, the other softly brushing the edge of her cape, just to make sure she was there.

'Hern's antlers, these packs are heavy,' Crom muttered as they paused by the jagged trunk of a huge Scots pine. Tansy grunted in agreement, but that was all the conversation they had. Podkin was scared of making any noise, just in case there was a Gorm crow sitting in a tree nearby. Besides, his pack didn't seem too bad. It only had a water bottle, some acorn bread and a blanket inside. He didn't fancy being lumbered with any more, just to help out.

The scent of the forest changed as they went further north. The pine slowly vanished, replaced by gentler, loamy smells of other trees: oak, beech, hazel. These trunks weren't so close together, their branches higher, and Podkin didn't get whacked in the face by twigs quite so much. He looked up, trying to see the moon in the sky, but there must have been thick cloud covering everything now. Not even a star to be seen. *Shame*, he thought. *I wanted to show Crom how Moonfyre worked.* But then, he wouldn't be able to see it anyway. Podkin felt a little cheated, until he realised that it was much worse for poor Crom, unable to share or join in with so much.

Hours later, when it felt like they had been walking *forever*, Crom brushed his fingers across one last tree and halted, making Podkin and Paz walk into the back of him. He pointed to the carved mark he had found, and turned to Mash. 'This is the rune for ending. Is that the edge of the forest?'

Podkin couldn't see anything but the shadows of trees, although the fact he could see anything at all meant it must be getting lighter.

'Yes,' said Mash. 'I think we're near Boneroot. Or at least, where Boneroot *was*.'

There was nothing left of the underground cavern where they'd met Crom. Just a gaping hole, thanks to the Gorm. Podkin remembered the evil rabbits, Shape and Quince, who had captured them there, and the flames and screaming when they had run for their lives. He had absolutely no desire to see that place again, empty hole or not.

'We camp here,' said Crom. 'We'll leave the forest tomorrow evening.'

Podkin had never heard such wonderful words. He wanted to collapse right there, but Mash put him to work, using Starclaw to cut branches from the trees. Tansy and Paz tied them together with vines to make two lean-to shelters up against the trunks of neighbouring oaks. They shovelled piles of dead leaves and rotten braches up against the outside to hide them, and then climbed in for a quick meal of acorn bread and some wilted dandelion leaves from Tansy's backpack.

'Tomorrow we'll forage for some fresh food,' Mash said, his mouth full of stale crumbs. 'Some watercress or mustard. Wild garlic shoots, maybe.'

'Thank the Goddess it's spring,' said Paz. 'I'm so sick of acorn bread.'

Podkin's stomach rumbled in agreement, and he tried to enjoy the thought of fresh, crunchy green salad, but his eyes were already closing. As the forest woke up to a misty dawn, he was fast asleep, snoring quietly in his nest of blankets.

*

He was having a dream about an earthquake shaking down the walls of his burrow and rocking him from side to side, when he woke up. Paz was nudging him, much more forcefully than she needed to.

'Whassa matter?' he managed to say. Mash was still fast asleep next to them, and from the other shelter, he could hear the sound of Crom's deep, rumbling snores. There was daylight outside, but it was fading. They had slept right through to evening time.

'Look at this!' Paz said, pointing to the roof of their lean-to shelter.

'What? Branches? Twigs?' Podkin couldn't see anything, certainly nothing worth being woken up from a nice sleep for.

'There!' Paz pointed again. 'Watch!'

Some of the branches they had cut were dusted green with the first buds of new growth. It was one of these Paz wanted him to see. A little cluster of crumpled leaves, almost ready to peep out into the world for the first time.

As Podkin watched, the bud trembled and the furled leaves twitched. They began to stretch and unfold, cracking out of their casing with tiny popping sounds. Podkin's mouth fell open as he saw the bright, fresh green of new oak leaves appear, spreading outwards in seconds, as if all the weeks of spring had been squashed into a few heartbeats.

More buds began to pop open all up and down the branch, and soon the whole thing was in full leaf. There were even shiny new acorns hanging down and brushing the ears of the sleeping Mash.

'What?' Podkin said. 'How?'

Paz held up Brigid's sickle. 'It's this,' she said. 'I was lying here, looking up at the branches, when I felt it tingling on my belt. When I grabbed hold of it, I could *feel* the power, Podkin. I could feel the leaves on the branches, wanting to grow.'

'Toasted turnips . . .' Podkin whispered.

'All I had to do was concentrate on the buds,' Paz continued, 'and they just popped out. That ivy down there too.' She pointed to where Mash's leg was sticking out of his blanket. His whole paw was wrapped all around with shiny green ivy leaves.

'Brigid never said that was the sickle's power, did she?' Podkin scratched the stump of his ear, trying to remember. 'I thought it only shone to tell her which plants were safe.'

'So did I,' said Paz. 'Maybe this is something new. Do you remember her telling us about the Balance? How the power of nature and the Gorm had to be equal? Maybe, because the Gorm are getting more powerful, the Goddess's Gifts are too.'

Podkin thought back to the battle at the Gorm camp. Right at the end, when Brigid had unleashed her powers to cover the place in a magical mist, he thought he'd seen tendrils of plants reach up from the ground and pull down the metal pillar that was part of the evil Gorm god, Gormalech. Could Brigid have done that as well, using the power of Ailfew? And then there was Starclaw – it had started 'speaking' to him much more lately. Zings and buzzes that tied in to what he was feeling or thinking. Maybe Paz was right: the Balance could be changing.

His sleepy brain was just beginning to puzzle it out when there came a shout of alarm from the other shelter.

Tansy! thought Podkin, and he and Paz dashed out into the forest to see what was wrong. Mash was a second behind them, but his foot was still wrapped in ivy, and he crashed to the floor in a cloud of leaves.

'What is it? What's happened?' Podkin reached the shelter first, and peered inside, drawing Starclaw as he moved. He half expected to see a Gorm crow, pecking at his friends with its evil metal beak – but instead there was Tansy, gaping at one of the backpacks they had brought with them.

It was open on the ground, and peering out of the top was a chubby little face with crumpled ears and wide green eyes.

'Puh-prise!' shouted Pook, beaming up at them all.

*

'Absolutely no way,' said Crom. 'We turn around and take him back, right now.'

'But then we've wasted a whole day,' said Tansy. 'Every second we lose could mean Comfrey is closer to death, or worse. Without her help, we'll never know how to find the hammer.'

'We can't take him with us.' Crom folded his arms in his best stubborn pose. 'Podkin and Paz have to be here, Brigid's always right about things like that. And they've more than proved themselves in the past.' (Podkin couldn't help puffing his chest out a little at *that*). 'But I won't risk Pook. Not where we're going. It's too dangerous for him.'

'We could send Podkin or Paz back with him,' Mash suggested. 'And the rest of us could carry on.'

'Didn't you hear Crom? Podkin and I need to be there,' said Paz, 'or the quest for the hammer will fail. Brigid said so.'

'We could leave him here,' said Tansy. 'Give him some food and tie him to a tree so he doesn't run off.'

'He's a baby, not a pet!' Podkin and Paz shouted the same thing together. Tansy shot them a nasty look and started packing up her gear.

'Well, we'd better decide one way or the other,' she said, over her shoulder. 'It's dusk now, and we need to move out of the forest.'

Pook had been watching them all closely and, realising they were thinking of sending him back to the warren, decided to give them some persuasion. He closed his eyes, threw his head back and screamed.

'Pook! Quiet!' Podkin hissed, thinking of all the Gorm scouts or crows that could be around.

'Make him hush!' Crom begged Paz, who knelt by Pook's side and tried to calm him down.

But there was no stopping the little rabbit. He paused to fill his lungs and then screamed again. Birds flew from the trees, squirrels scampered for cover. Every living thing for miles around would soon know where they were.

'All right, all right!' Crom bent down to talk to the wailing Pook. 'You can come along! I'll carry you myself! Just be quiet, for Goddess's sake!'

There was instant silence. Pook grinned up at Crom, as if nothing had ever been wrong, and reached out his arms to be picked up. Crom swung him on to his shoulders, muttering something about wailing kittens being the death of him, while the others all stared on in surprise.

Tansy was shaking her head, looking far from happy. 'This is supposed to be a secret mission, not a child's tea party.' Podkin gave her his best glare, but had to admit he wasn't happy either. He'd been sad to leave Pook, but at least he'd known his baby brother was safe. Now all three of them were in danger – again.

Feeling even more uneasy than before, the little group headed off into the twilight, and out of the shelter of Grimheart forest.

CHAPTER SEVEN

Assassin

Once they had left the forest, Podkin soon realised how vulnerable they were. There was open space all around. Wide, grassy meadows, broken here and there by the odd copse of trees or cluster of gorse bushes. If the wrong eyes were watching, they would be very visible as they hurried across the landscape. A cluster of hooded rabbits, headed straight into danger.

They continued their path north, zigging and zagging to make the most of any cover they could find. Podkin came to hate the open pasture, counting the steps between each bit of hedge or bush that would help hide them. He realised this must be how his ancestors once felt: always waiting for the snap of a fox's jaws or the sound of falcon wings swooping down on them from above.

They had decided to skirt around any warrens on the way to Applecross, just in case the Gorm were there. The nearest one to the forest was called Frog Wallop, and by the end of the night they were getting close to it. Mash pointed to a small wood, nestling between two little hills.

'If we can reach that,' he said, 'we could camp there for the day. We can make shelters like before, and there might be some good food around.'

It sounded like an excellent plan to Podkin, and they all doubled their pace, trying to reach the trees before the sun came up. When they were a hundred metres or so away, they used up the last of their energy in a mad dash, desperate to be under cover.

Camp was made very quickly, right in the middle of the little wood, in the hollow trunk of a wide ancient yew tree. It was a bit cramped, all squashed inside with a blanket hiding them from sight, but everyone was just happy to be hidden once more.

They felt even better when Mash appeared after a scouting trip. He had a bundle of mushrooms, some wild asparagus and more dandelion leaves.

'Could we make a fire to cook some soup?' Podkin asked, his stomach making him forget his fear of the Gorm for a moment.

'Soop!' said Pook, licking his lips.

'Best not,' said Crom. 'We were lucky to go all night without seeing any sign of the enemy. It would be stupid to tempt fate.'

Rats' whiskers, Podkin scolded himself. *Think before you speak next time. Of course you can't cook soup when you're hiding from a bunch of iron-clad monsters.* He nibbled on some raw mushrooms, and tried to ignore his rumbling tummy.

Before long the simple meal was gone, and the group of rabbits huddled together, their furry bodies stuffing the empty tree trunk to the brim. Mash went off to keep first watch and Podkin made himself comfortable. He had his head on Paz's back and Pook's ears were in his face, but he didn't mind.

It was actually very cosy.

'See you all in the morning . . . I mean, the evening,' he said, but was asleep before anyone could answer.

*

'The first one to move a whisker is a dead rabbit.'

It was a voice he'd never heard before. Low – growling – female, possibly? – and it made Podkin snap awake instantly. Not the half-asleep, bleary-headed wakening of the evening before, either. His eyes were popping, his ear pricked and every bristle of fur on his neck was bolt upright.

The first thing he saw was a strange figure standing over them where they lay. It had long grey robes, a bladed weapon in its hand, and a skull for a face – gleaming white bone, carved all over with whorls and spirals.

Everyone in the tree trunk was awake too. Crom was frozen in the act of reaching for his spear, Tansy had her teeth gritted in anger, and Pook and Paz looked terrified.

From the corner of his eye, Podkin could see the clearing outside their tree. Mash was lying there, not dead – thank the Goddess – but tied hand and foot.

There were shadowy shapes amongst the woods: more strangers holding weapons. Not the bulky, spiked figures of Gorm, though. Something else? Something worse?

'Who are you?' Podkin heard himself squeak.

Quicker than a blink, their captor reached down to grab his ear, yanking it hard. The bone-faced monster held its blade to Podkin's throat, pushing the jagged edge through his fur and into his skin.

'I'll ask the questions, earless one,' it hissed. The words had an accent he hadn't heard before, but the voice was definitely female. Podkin looked up, seeing that the skull face was just a mask. Through the eyeholes he could see black fur and a pair of cold, slate-grey eyes. *At least it's a rabbit, and not some kind of demon*, was all Podkin could think.

'Leave the child alone,' said Crom, his voice a growl. 'Threaten me, if you dare.'

'Be careful what you ask for, greyfur. Do you know what I am?'

'I think so,' Crom replied. 'Are you wearing a bone mask?'

The rabbit took her knife away from Podkin's

throat for a moment and tapped the blade against her mask. *Tchk, tchk, tchk.* Crom nodded his head. When he spoke again, his voice was softer, less angry.

'Everyone do what this rabbit says. Don't try anything stupid.'

'Very wise,' said the rabbit. She let go of Podkin's ear and he tumbled on to Paz's lap. Despite Crom's warning, he was tempted to draw Starclaw and give the masked rabbit a scare. Chop her sword in half, or slice off her stupid mask. She didn't look that dangerous – apart from the scary bone face, of course – she was only a fraction taller than Tansy and as skinny as a starved weasel. Why was Crom so frightened?

'Now,' she said. 'Who are you, and why are you here? Don't you know this land is run by the Gorm now?'

Podkin was about to say something about them being on a dangerous mission, when Tansy spoke up. 'We're from Applecross warren,' she said. 'We're fleeing the Gorm. Trying to find somewhere safe.'

The masked rabbit pointed her sword at Tansy.

'You, maybe, are from Applecross. These others: no. A dwarf from the mountains, a grey rabbit from the forest and three baby field rabbits. Besides, you are going *towards* Applecross, not away. We watched you last night.'

So much for travelling unnoticed, Podkin thought. *If they saw us, who else did?* Could there be Gorm riders on their way to them right now?

'We mean you no harm,' said Crom. 'We have a task to do at Applecross. We can't tell you what, but trust us when we say if you are enemies of the Gorm, then we are on the same side.'

There was a long moment of silence. Podkin could see the masked rabbit's eyes looking at each of them in turn, sizing them up and wondering whether to release them or kill them where they lay.

Finally she jumped down from the tree to the clearing floor, landing as silently as a wildcat, just behind Mash. Her sword swished through the air and around her head in a maze of spirals, and a scream began to form in Podkin's throat. She was going to chop Mash to pieces, before starting on the rest of them!

Podkin heard Paz gasp as the sword came down, faster than a blink, slicing cleanly through the rope binding Mash's paws. The little rabbit quickly jumped to his feet, rubbing his wrists and looking very annoyed.

Did this mean they were safe? Paz had already started clambering out of the tree, so he guessed it did. Podkin followed. By the time they were standing in the clearing, the masked rabbit's friends had stepped into the open.

They made a strange bunch.

There were two others besides the masked one: a sinewy, ginger-furred rabbit with nervous gold-flecked eyes, dressed in the most beautiful woven cloak Podkin had ever seen; and a rabbit that could only be a bard. He had smoke-grey fur, shaven and dyed into swirling patterns. The insides of his ears were tattooed with more swirls and pierced with two huge wooden discs. Through his nose was a silver ring and he held a carved oak staff, strung with feathers, beads and bones. When he saw Podkin staring at him, he bowed low and smiled.

'These are my fellows,' said the masked rabbit.

'Vetch of Golden Brook and Yarrow, bard of nowhere in particular. I am Zarza.'

'A bonedancer,' said Crom, and both Tansy and Mash drew a sharp breath. Podkin only frowned. *What under the earth was a bonedancer? And why was she so scary?*

While Podkin was puzzling, Crom made their introductions. The two groups agreed to share a meal together before they moved on, although neither of them was prepared to say where they were going just yet. Food was dished out on to a blanket in silence, and they all sat around it, nervously eying each other.

'Well,' said Yarrow, the bard. 'This is all terribly awkward, isn't it? Perhaps I should break the ice with a song?' Even though he was fairly young – no more than twenty summers, Podkin reckoned – there was an old-fashioned, theatrical showmanship in everything he did and said.

'As long as it's not too loud,' said Zarza. She was feeding dandelion leaves through a slit in the front of her mask, silently nibbling them without pausing to take it off.

'Very well.' Yarrow stood and cleared his throat

before beginning to sing. His voice was soft, yet clear and beautiful. It seemed to blend with the evening sounds of the woods: the rustling trees, the roosting birds, the wind sighing through the branches. Podkin recognised the words: it was a song about Lupen, the first rabbit, who ended up in the moon. The tune was different to the one he knew, but it fitted the song even better. When he had finished, the rabbits quietly applauded. Pook, who had been staring with an open mouth all the way through the song, quietly got up and toddled across the blanket to sit at Yarrow's feet, staring up at him like he was some kind of magical vision.

'Thank you,' said Paz. 'That was lovely.'

'You're very welcome,' said Yarrow, patting Pook on the head. 'It's nice to have an appreciative audience, for a change.'

'Now that the ice is broken, perhaps we should share some tales about ourselves?' It was the ginger-furred rabbit, Vetch, who had spoken. He sat, wrapped in his glorious cloak, staring at them in turn. His golden eyes flicked from face to face, his mouth curled in a half smile.

'I'll start, shall I?' Nobody answered him, or even glanced his way, although he didn't seem to notice. Podkin began to feel a little sorry for him. 'My name, as you know, is Vetch. I was the advisor to Chief Gildus of Golden Brook warren. I don't know if you've ever been there, but it is quite famous. We have seams of pure gold running through the very walls of our longburrow. Sculptures and fountains everywhere. The place is a marvel.

'Or it *was* a marvel, I should say, for the Gorm came and ruined it all. I daresay there's nothing of beauty left in it now. I believe I was the only survivor, the only one to escape. I had been wandering for weeks before I met these two, and they have agreed to escort me to safety.'

'We agreed nothing of the sort,' said Zarza, halfway through a dandelion leaf.

'I offered to pay you handsomely,' said Vetch.

'I don't want your gold. I don't want you slowing me down. You're only with us because I hate the Gorm more than you.'

'Yes,' said Vetch. 'Well. They *don't* seem to be escorting me to safety. Rather, I am staying with them until I find somewhere safer. Which amounts to the same thing, don't you think?'

He stared at them again with those gleaming, nervous eyes. He seemed desperate for someone to like him. A bit too desperate, perhaps. Podkin gave him a little smile anyway, and was rewarded with a beaming grin and a bow.

'How fascinating. Shall I go next?' Yarrow was still being gawped at by Pook, although he seemed to be enjoying the attention. He performed an elaborate bow that made Pook chortle and wiggle. 'Yarrow is my name: a wandering bard, collector of tales and singer of songs. I have been travelling Gotland since the Gorm's arrival, gathering stories and recording the history of those foul beasts with my phenomenal memory –' he tapped his head –'so that one day I may sing of their evil and how it was defeated.' He paused for dramatic effect.

'Except it doesn't look like it's really going to be defeated at the moment, which is a tragic shame. Our lovely Zarza here seems to be giving it a shot, though, which is why I am following her. One day, her tale will be famous, her name known by rabbitkind throughout the Five Realms ... should there be anyone left alive to sing it, of course.'

The bonedancer stared across the circle at Yarrow with a look that could have wilted a radish. 'I don't *want* to be famous, singing rabbit. I just want to kill Gorm.'

'And you are so terribly good at it, my dear.' Yarrow sat back down and let Pook curl up on his lap.

Podkin looked at the other rabbits to see who would speak next. Zarza was ignoring everyone completely, and all of his friends had their lips firmly closed. *Well, if nobody else is going to say anything* ... he thought.

'I am Podkin, son of Lopkin, once of Munbury. We've all come from Dark Hollow: a warren hidden in the middle of Grimheart forest. We're on a quest to find the sacred hammer of Applecross so we can use it to—'

'Podkin!' Paz shouted, jumping up from her seat and grabbing him by the arm. 'You're not supposed to tell everybody that, you ferret-faced lump! Have you got turnips for brains or something?'

'But they were all telling stories ...'

'It doesn't matter! They could be Gorm spies, for all you know, and now you've blabbed everything!'

Podkin blushed crimson under his fur again. He had only wanted to join in. Was telling these rabbits so bad? What if they could help them find the hammer?

He looked across at Crom. The big rabbit's face was like a thundercloud. Paz's was just as bad, and Tansy was shaking her head at him. The new rabbits, on the other hand, were looking very interested all of a sudden. What had he done?

'Tell us more about this hammer,' Zarza said. Her grey eyes gleamed from the hollows of her mask.

'I'd probably better not,' said Podkin, and he sat down quickly, pulling his cloak hood up and trying to vanish from sight as much as possible.

'Why don't *you* tell *us* something?' Paz asked, turning her glare on the masked rabbit. 'What under earth is a bonedancer, anyway? And why is everyone so scared of you?'

Podkin silently thanked her for changing the subject.

Zarza stared back at Paz with those eyes like

frosty granite. To her credit, she didn't even flinch. Podkin got the impression that the bonedancer was smiling underneath her mask. 'Are you scared of me, little field rabbit?'

Paz stood, hands on hips and chest puffed out. 'No, I'm not. I've faced worse than you, even though I might be "little". I've fought off Gorm more times than you have, I bet, and *I* don't go around being rude to rabbits I've only just met!'

Podkin was surprised to hear Zarza chuckle. She bowed her head to Paz, and made a gesture with an open palm that looked like an offering of respect. It seemed to Podkin that his sister had passed some kind of test.

'Apologies for my rudeness,' Zarza said. 'I'm sure your big friend can tell you all about my order.'

'Bonedancers are hired assassins,' said Crom. 'Paid killers. The best in the Five Realms, if you can afford them. They come from a temple in Thrianta called Spinestone. Only women can join them, and they serve Nixha, the goddess of death.'

'And only those who have risen to the rank of sister are allowed to hire out their skills,' Zarza

139

replied, continuing to stare at Paz. 'I am but a novice myself.'

'A novice?' Podkin forgot he was trying to be invisible. 'Does that mean you're still learning how to kill people?'

'Oh, I know all about killing, little one-ear. In fact, we bonedancers must kill something every day. The goddess Nixha requires it.'

Podkin gulped. 'Have you killed something today then?'

'Not yet.' Zarza winked at him, making him huddle further into his cloak. Then she reached for a leather pouch at her belt, dipped her long fingers inside it and pulled out a little green beetle. As Podkin watched in horror, she twisted off the tiny creature's head, then winked at him again.

'That's better,' she said.

'How cruel!' said Paz, still standing in her tough-rabbit stance.

'If you became a bonedancer, you wouldn't think so.'

Paz had no reply to that. Had she just been made an offer? Or was Zarza simply teasing her? Podkin couldn't work out which it was, but somehow he couldn't imagine his sister in a bone mask, swishing swords through the air. Then again, it might actually suit her very well, especially when she was in one of her early-morning moods.

Soon after that, they packed away the remains of their meal and prepared to leave. As they were tucking their supplies neatly into their packs, Podkin noticed Zarza drawing Crom aside for a quiet word. The urge to find out what they were saying overcame his fear of the masked rabbit and her sharp sword. He started to edge a bit closer.

'Curiosity killed the rabbit,' warned Paz, looking up from her packing.

'But what are they talking about? Do you think Crom is going to hire her to kill the Gorm?'

'What's he going to pay her with? Pine cones?' Paz shook her head. 'I bet she's wanting to know about the hammer. You really should learn to keep your mouth shut.'

'And you should learn to ... to ...' Podkin was still thinking of something horrid to say when Crom finished talking and came over to them.

'Well,' he said. 'It looks like we've got some travelling companions. They want to come with us as far as Applecross.'

'But Crom!' Paz raised her voice as loud as she dared. 'They're just after the hammer! They heard what Podkin said, and now they want the Gift for themselves!'

Crom shrugged. 'Maybe. But I know a bit about bonedancers. They're not interested in treasure or booty, apart from their fee, of course. Novices like Zarza have special quests to do before they can become proper sisters of the order. Zarza's is to do as much damage to the Gorm as possible. I think she'll be very useful to us.'

'But what about the others?' Podkin asked. 'How can we trust them?'

'Yarrow's just after a good tale,' said Crom. 'And as for that Vetch ... well, I trust him about as far as I can throw a giant rat. We'll have to put up with him, though, if we want Zarza's help. Mentioning our mission might have been a good move after all, Podkin.'

Before anything else could be said, the blind

rabbit walked off to ready the others, leaving Podkin lost in thought and Paz quietly seething. Dusk had fallen, and the sky above the wood was filling with the flitting shapes of hungry bats snatching plump moths out of the air. Podkin looked out on to the open plains between him and Applecross warren. Plains he was now about to walk through in the dark, with a group of rabbits that might be waiting for the perfect chance to knock him over the head and steal his magic treasures. He clutched Starclaw tight and felt it judder in response. Moonfyre was still pinned inside his jerkin, pressing into his fur. Could he use it to jump through a shadow, right back to his mother's side in Dark Hollow warren?

But the night sky was blank and cloudy, the moon nowhere to be seen.

INTERLUDE

I t is morning, and the bard wakes to find a pale spring mist filling the little valley where he and Rue camped for the night. It has coated his blanket with dew, and little droplets like diamonds hang in his whiskers.

He had told his tale until well after sundown, sitting by the fireside with Rue staring up at him with twinkling eyes, much in the same way that he had once stared up at Yarrow on a darkening evening, in a little wood a long, long time ago.

Not that Rue knew that. The little rabbit was just lost in the story, his face warmed by a crackling fire, the cold, empty darkness of night at his back. Just the way stories had first been told, before things like warrens and hearths were invented.

Groaning at his stiff joints, the bard shrugs off his blanket and stretches out his creaking limbs. Rue is still sound asleep: just a twitching nose and the tip of a speckled ear poking out from his nest of cloak and blankets. *How cute*, thinks the bard, surprising himself with his paternal feelings. But they don't last long.

He wonders how best to wake a little rabbit up. Throw some water over him? Give him a good kick? In the end he builds up the fire and starts to make some porridge for breakfast, banging the pans together as loudly as he can.

'Is it morning?' A muffled voice comes from the blanket-nest.

'Yes it is, you lazy lump. And we have to be off if we want to make the start of the festival.'

The Festival of Clarion. All the noise, the bustle, the songs and the stories. It has been years since he last went. Was that the year Ogbert the Bold won the High Bard's cup for his ballad singing? Or was it when his friend Finwald ate those spicy Thriantan radishes and couldn't speak for a week? He'd been to so many now, they all blurred into each other. Mostly he remembered there being far too many rabbits for his liking. All the bumping and jostling. The singing and shouting, the drinking and feasting.

'I can't wait to see the festival. Is it fun?' Rue's voice is full of innocent excitement.

'Oh,' says the bard, trying not to sound too fed up. 'It's wonderful. Simply glorious. Especially if you like lying awake until four in the morning, listening to several hundred drunken bards all trying to sing different songs at once. Now be quiet and eat your porridge.'

*

They set off soon after, breathing in the heavy, cold air of the mist, working their way up the hillside until they are above it – a ghostly white blanket laying across the grasslands as far as the eye can see.

The trek up the steep downs has kept Rue out of breath, but as soon as they pause at the top, blinking in the sudden sunshine, the questions start.

'So,' he says. 'Bonedancers. Is there really such a thing?'

'There is,' says the bard, leaning on his staff, trying to get his breath back. Rue doesn't hear him mutter, 'Unfortunately.'

'What, still? In real life?'

'In real life,' says the bard. He gestures off to the east. 'Over there, past the grasslands and the swamps, their temple still stands.'

'And people can hire them? If they want somebody killed, I mean?'

The bard nods and shudders. He scans the wide empty downs around them, as if checking for something, then pulls his cloak tighter around his shoulders. 'Let's stop talking about this, shall we? We really should be getting on.'

'Why don't you want to talk about it?' Rue asks, but the bard has already started walking. He skips after him, pelting the old rabbit with questions, but the bard's lips are firmly closed. In the end they walk in silence for a while, watching as the sun slowly burns off the mist around them, gradually revealing the land beneath like a Bramblemas Day present being unwrapped.

It is getting near to lunchtime when Rue stops

them with a shout: 'Rabbits! On the path before us! Do you think they're going to the festival too?'

The bard squints against the sunshine. There are two rabbits up ahead, cloaked, with walking staffs and packs. Could be simple travellers, but on this day and going in this direction, they probably *are* bards, heading for the festival. The bard pauses to draw his hood up, pulling it down over his eyes.

It soon becomes clear that the two figures are waiting for them. As they get closer, Rue spots the dyed fur and tattooed ears that give them away.

'Bards! Real bards!' he squeaks.

'What d'you think I am? Chopped parsley?' The bard pulls his hood down further. He was hoping to slip into the festival un-noticed, lost amongst all the noise and bustle.

'Well met, fellow travellers!' One of the figures waves. It is a female rabbit, young, with brindled fur and only a feather or two tied to her staff. Newly trained then – nobody the bard has ever seen before.

'Well met,' he replies, keeping his eyes down.

'A fellow minstrel!' The other rabbit speaks. This one is older and he has a harp slung over his shoulder. The bard thinks he recognises him from somewhere. A springtime in the past, perhaps. 'Are you heading for the festival?'

'Yes!' Rue hops up and down. 'Are you going too?'

'We are,' says the lady rabbit. 'Shall we walk together?'

'Oh,' says the bard, ignoring Rue's excited squealing. 'We would only slow you down. Besides, we were just about to stop for lunch. I am sure we'll meet you again, at the festival ground.'

'That's a shame,' says the elder rabbit, nodding towards the bard's bead and feather-covered staff. 'We were hoping for a chance to trade stories. Especially with one so experienced as yourself. Haven't I seen you before? You aren't Wulf the Wanderer, are you?'

'Me?' says the bard. He notices Rue staring up at him, ears twitching away. 'Oh no, not I. I'm just from a little warren in Enderby. I don't usually make it to the festival, what with my bad legs, but my little lad wanted to see it so ...'

'Funny,' says the elder rabbit. 'I could have sworn you were him. Your voice even sounds the same.'

'Nonsense, nonsense,' says the bard, coughing

and spluttering a little. 'You must be mistaken. I could never hope to be as renowned as Wulf. Didn't he win the High Bard's cup once or twice?'

'Seven times,' says the rabbit. 'I saw him perform, once. He had the same staff as you and everything.'

'Really? What a coincidence.' The bard makes a show of putting his pack down and looking for something inside it. 'Now, if you'll excuse us, my poor tummy is in need of feeding. We would offer to share, but we don't really have enough to go round ...'

'Don't worry.' The elder rabbit frowns down at the huddled back of the bard, digging around in his pack. 'We'll be on our way. See you at the festival.'

'Yes, yes,' says the bard, not looking up. 'See you there.'

The two rabbits leave, heading along the eastward path. Rue watches them with sad eyes.

'Why couldn't we have gone with them? They might have taught me some songs, or how to play the harp.'

'Harps are for show-offs,' says the bard. He spreads a blanket on the floor and starts laying out wooden plates and packets of food. 'Learn to tell stories properly first, then you can start farting around with instruments.'

'He knew you, didn't he?' Rue puts his hands on his hips and glares at the bard. 'He kept saying you were Wulf the Wanderer, and you kept pretending you weren't.'

'Rubbish,' says the bard. 'Come on, have some lunch.'

'Have you really won the High Bard's cup seven times? Why wouldn't you tell him who you were? Are you trying to hide from somebody?'

'Aaah!' the bard shouts, making Rue jump in the air. A long silence follows while the bard tugs at his beard and Rue tries not to cry.

'Look,' says the bard eventually. 'I'm sorry I shouted, but you're just asking too many questions. Come and have some lunch, and perhaps I'll continue the story of Podkin for you.'

'All right,' says Rue, quietly. He sits down on the blanket and puts some smoked parsnips on his plate. His questions will keep for later.

'That's a good rabbit,' says the bard. He sighs, as if relieved. 'Now. Where were we?'

CHAPTER EIGHT

Dancing

The strange party left the copse of trees as darkness fell, heading northwest to Applecross – nine huddled shadows in the gloom.

Zarza led the group at a swift pace, Paz trotting behind as close as she dared, itching to ask about her mysterious order. She finally managed to catch a moment to whisper, 'What you said about becoming a bonedancer . . .' She had to hop and skip to keep up with Zarza. 'Can anyone be one?'

'Interested, are we?' Zarza kept her gaze forward, but sounded amused.

'Not really. Well, just curious.'

From his place back in the line, Podkin could see his sister's ears twitching. That only happened when she was embarrassed.

'Only women can be bonedancers,' said Zarza. 'First daughters, usually. The bravest and strongest are selected. There are tests.'

'Tests?'

'I think you would do well.'

Zarza strode on then, outpacing Paz, who fell back to where Podkin was walking, a smug grin on her face.

'I think you'd make a great bonedancer as well,' Podkin said.

'You do?'

He waited for her grin to grow even bigger. 'Yes, sis. With one of those masks on all day, no one would have to look at your stupid face.'

Podkin skipped out of the way, but not quickly enough to avoid a flick on his good ear. It stung like a wasp; perhaps she *would* be a good assassin after all.

Pook had left his usual spot on Crom's shoulders, and was now riding on Yarrow, the bard. Podkin could hear them quietly singing to each other. Yarrow would whisper the first few lines of a song, and Pook would warble them back in his little nonsense language.

'Ooh ooh, boo bah, eegy eegy ooh.'

Crom hadn't said anything about this new arrangement, but he was stomping a bit more than usual. Could he be jealous? Podkin scurried up to walk beside him, just in case, and was rewarded with a brush of the big rabbit's fingers across his head. Neither of them needed to say anything.

The other rabbits followed behind, Mash bringing up the rear. Vetch, wrapped in his exotic cloak, sidled up to Podkin at one point, giving him a nervous smile. His golden eyes kept darting to the dagger on Podkin's hip.

'I must say, that is an unusual weapon you have.'

'It was my father's,' said Podkin. He didn't want to be rude, but thought it best that Starclaw remained a secret, at least until he knew more about these new rabbits.

'The blind rabbit?' Vetch asked, with a tilt of his head. 'Is he your father?'

'My father's dead,' said Podkin, the words as hard to say as ever. 'Crom was his friend. He looks after us now.'

'Oh, I am sorry.' Vetch looked mortified at his mistake. 'Please do forgive me. I had no idea ...'

'It's all right,' Podkin began, when he noticed Crom's head had turned in their direction. Crom scowled at Vetch, then gave a growl, which sent the ginger rabbit scurrying. Podkin looked back and gave him an apologetic smile. He understood why Crom wanted to be cautious, but at the same time felt sympathy for Vetch. Everyone seemed to be unkind to him. Was it because he wasn't much use as a fighter, or was it some other, grown-up reason Podkin didn't understand? He scratched at his missing ear and wondered about it as they marched on.

They walked like that for what felt like hours, through a grey, lonely landscape. Clouds covered the sky, and it seemed like they were lost in a world of nothing. Only the occasional shadow of a hunting owl, gliding overhead, broke up the emptiness.

The silence, the blankness: Podkin had begun to wonder if he wasn't stuck in a dream, his body still back in Dark Hollow, curled up in his little bed. The illusion was only broken when Zarza suddenly dropped to the ground, hissing an alarm call back to everyone else.

Crom dropped too, reaching out a hand to pull Podkin down next to him. Within seconds, everyone was pressed flat to the earth, blades of grass tickling their noses.

'What is it?' Podkin whispered in Crom's ear. 'Is it the Gorm?'

'Hush,' Crom whispered back. 'There's voices.'

Podkin strained to listen, pricking up his one remaining ear, but he couldn't hear anything except the gentle rustling of wind in the grass and the breathing of the rabbits in his party. He noticed Zarza and Paz had started to inch forwards, staying close to the ground, and he began to follow them.

They crept along, painfully slowly, until they reached the top of a slope. Beyond it, the land dropped away into a valley, which had been completely hidden in the darkness. There were copses of trees down there, freshly ploughed fields and the glowing light of lanterns.

Podkin held his breath and edged next to Paz and Zarza, keeping his ear tucked down as he peered over the edge.

The light came from the open door of a small burrow. A little family farm, probably. It was too tiny to be a warren of any kind. Podkin could hear the voices now, although they were nothing more than murmurs. Someone was whimpering or crying – and was that a shout?

There was a sudden *crash* that made Podkin jump, and something came flying out of the burrow door, smashing it wide open. It rolled on the floor, then began to twitch and tremble. A rabbit.

Cries and screams came from the burrow then, and a figure stepped out into the night, walking towards the fallen rabbit. A bulky, hunched figure, studded all over with twisted shards and spikes.

'Gorm!' Podkin gasped and snatched at Paz's arm. He hadn't seen them since they had rescued their mother, and now all the terror of that night came rushing back at once. He felt himself beginning to tremble and shake, his fur standing up on end.

'Shh!' Zarza hissed. She had silently drawn her

weapon: a thin, wicked-looking thing with a curved bronze blade and handle of carved bone. Podkin looked to Paz for comfort, but she was just as scared as him, unable to take her eyes off the armoured shape in front of them.

As they watched, the Gorm heaved the fallen rabbit up by its ears. It said something in a harsh, grating voice, and a second figure stepped out of the burrow and into the pool of yellow light cast by the open door. Behind them they dragged another rabbit, who was desperately trying to cling to three crying little children.

'I know what you're thinking, Zarza,' came Crom's voice. He had edged up to the brow of the slope along with the rest of the party. 'But we can't risk getting involved. Our mission is to get to Applecross.'

'*I* can get involved,' whispered Zarza. 'They are Gorm, and my goddess demands that they be stopped.'

'Are you mad? I can hear at least two of them. You'll never bring them down by yourself.'

'I have to try,' Zarza replied. 'That is why I am here.'

To his horror, Podkin realised she was going to charge at the Gorm – all by herself. Yarrow was watching with wide eyes, drinking in every detail for a story or song, should he survive.

'Crom,' said Mash. 'We can't just leave those rabbits down there. The Gorm will slaughter them.' Podkin noticed that the dwarf rabbit had his blowpipe ready, his fingers pulling a dart from the pouches on his chest. He had once been part of a travelling troupe of acrobats that hunted Gorm in their spare time, and Podkin wondered how many times Mash had been in this sort of situation.

'I know it seems harsh,' Crom hissed. 'But we have children to protect. We also have a mission to complete. If we die here, who will get the hammer?'

'This won't take long,' said Zarza, and before anyone could stop her, she was up and running, down the slope towards the Gorm.

'Sorry,' said Mash, and then he was up too, scampering into the dark with his blowpipe at his lips.

'Hern's antlers!' Crom cursed. He grabbed Yarrow by the shoulder. 'Keep the children safe,' he said. 'If anything happens to us, run south.' With Tansy by his side, the blind warrior jumped up and charged after the others.

'Podkin!' Paz cried. 'What do we do?'

Podkin couldn't answer. His eyes were fixed on the battle down below, his breath caught in his throat.

*

The Gorm had been too busy to hear the approach of their attackers, caught up in the screams of the poor farmer, his wife and children. Zarza was upon them first – grey flowing robes melting out of nowhere, as if the twilight itself had come to life.

She cartwheeled into the first Gorm, striking him in the head with both feet. He staggered backwards, but then brought his weapon up quickly, ready to fight, and that was when Podkin understood why Zarza's order were called bone*dancers*.

She flowed and streamed around the massive Gorm, who swiped and slashed at her in a frenzy. He might as well have been fighting a plume of smoke. Zarza flipped and twirled – in the air, on the ground and everywhere in between. It was more of a performance than a fight, and Podkin was transfixed.

While that was going on, Mash had reached the second Gorm. The tiny rabbit began darting around its feet, trying to get a clear shot at the open eyeholes in the Gorm's helmet.

The creature threw down the farmer's wife and began to swipe at Mash with its sword. It only managed a few swings before Crom's spear hit it in the chest, denting the armour then bouncing aside. It was followed a second later by Crom, flying in with a double-footed kick that sent the armoured monster smashing through a wooden fence and into a field.

Now the quiet night was full of clashing metal. Fast-moving iron and bronze glinted in the burrow's lamplight

'Podkin!' Paz was calling him again, shaking his arm. 'We have to do something!'

'Oh no you don't,' said Yarrow. 'You children stay right here with me. And get yourselves ready to run.' The confident smiling bard was gone. Yarrow's voice was strained, his eyes wide and scared.

'The Gifts, Podkin. Can we use them?'

Podkin looked at his sister. Starclaw was useless against the Gorm armour. He had once used it to chop a tree down on to their heads, but there was nothing around them now but open farmland. He thought of the brooch, but there wasn't even a sliver of moon in the sky. All he could do was stare at Paz, shaking his head, helpless.

'I *can't* just sit here!' Paz shouted, and before he or Yarrow could stop her, she pushed herself up and ran towards the fighting.

'Paz!' Podkin shouted. He went to follow her, but Yarrow had tight hold of his cloak. He looked around for Vetch, thinking the ginger rabbit might help him, but he was nowhere to be seen.

'I'm sorry, Podkin,' Yarrow said. 'I can't let you go down there. You'll be cut to pieces, or I will, if your big friend survives.'

Podkin struggled for a moment, but the bard would not let him go. Pook was crying out for him. All Podkin could do was to take his little brother from Yarrow's shoulders, and hold him tight as they both stared down in horror at the farm.

*

Zarza was still somersaulting and twirling around the iron Gorm, like ink dropped into water. Now she threw things as she danced: bone darts with black-feathered flights. They peppered the Gorm's head, some thudding into the flesh of its open mouth, some slipping through the holes in its helmet to the soft red eyes beneath. The thing gave a horrible scream and then collapsed with a crash of tearing metal.

The others were not doing so well. The second Gorm had picked itself up, and was furiously swinging its broadsword in wide, sweeping arcs. Mash was firing dart after dart at the Gorm's helmet, but they all seemed to be pinging off. The iron-clad warrior was keeping his head moving, making the weak spots in his armour as hard a target as possible.

Crom had short swords in both hands now, and was blocking blows as best he could. Tansy was lying on the floor nearby, clutching her left leg and grimacing. At least she was still alive, but for how much longer?

As Podkin stared helplessly, he saw Paz run into the scene, holding something in her hand.

'Get back!' Zarza shouted, on the way to help the others. Paz ignored her. She held the thing she was carrying up high.

Ailfew. The sickle, Podkin realised. Paz dropped to both knees, the magic sickle held out before her. *She'll have her eyes closed*, Podkin thought, *focusing on the growing things around her.*

But what was there apart from grass? How could that stop an armoured warrior? He had visions of the Gorm spotting his sister – cutting her down and taking Ailfew.

'Come on, moon!' he shouted up at the sky. 'Goddess, where is the moon?'

It didn't matter, though. Paz – or Brigid's – magic had found something to work on. The farmer must have planted pumpkin seeds in his field. Beans too, and perhaps the tiny, weedling sprouts of brambles. Tendrils and shoots of all kinds began to burst out of the soft, open earth and creep their way towards the Gorm.

The warrior didn't notice at first, it was too busy closing in on its victims. The twining pumpkin and beanstalks began to wind their way up its legs, around its body and neck, growing thicker and tougher by the second.

Before Zarza could even join the attack, the Gorm

was held in place. It hadn't realised until too late. Now it couldn't even swing its sword to free itself because its arms and body were choked with thick green ropes. Podkin watched as it struggled and cursed, trying to break free, but the vines were pouring from the ground now, looping over each other in a tide of leaves that seemed as if it was never going to stop.

At last, there was silence. The battle had frozen mid-flow, the Gorm, Zarza, the farmers . . . everyone was staring at Paz, who was still kneeling on the ground, holding out the sickle.

Silently, she stood up, tucking her Gift back into her cloak – but it was too late now. Everyone had seen the magic, and they all knew what it meant.

Podkin didn't care, he was just glad his sister was safe. Finally breaking free of Yarrow's grasp, he ran down to her, still holding Pook in his arms.

*

Afterwards, they all gathered in the tiny farm-burrow. It was just a small room, hollowed out of the earth and filled with simple wooden furniture. A stove, a table, some chairs, a family bed, and now several stunned rabbits.

The farmer and his wife were huddled in a corner, trying to comfort their children. Across the room, Paz was talking to Yarrow, while Crom and Mash were tending to the wounded Tansy. Vetch had appeared from nowhere, and Podkin wondered where he'd come from. He definitely hadn't been amongst the fighting, but there had been too much going on to notice. Hiding, maybe? Waiting for a chance to help out?

Zarza was the only one still outside the burrow. She had sent them all away while she finished off the trapped Gorm. 'You don't want to see this,' she had said to him, and she was right. He'd had a glimpse of the captured monster, even seen her prise its helmet off. What was underneath was no longer a rabbit. The toxic metal of their god Gormalech had spread through its body, taking over every cell. Podkin had seen a flash of rust-red eyes, bulging veins turned black with poison and bare patches of fur where the skin underneath looked almost scaled, like a metal lizard. Even the briefest sight had made his stomach churn, and he had hurried inside as quickly as he could.

The thing hadn't screamed or shouted for help in the end. It just stood there, bound with vines and leaves, panting and gnashing its teeth. Like some horrid version of the Green Rabbit of Lupen's Day. Podkin wondered if perhaps the power of the plants was hurting it? Maybe it poisoned them like their iron poisoned the Goddess?

He would never know. There were some quiet, gurgling noises from the night outside, and then Zarza stepped in through the door, wiping her blade clean with a black silk cloth. She silently surveyed the room, and Podkin wondered what would happen next.

'It has to be,' Yarrow was saying. 'But the sickle of Redwater was lost years ago! How did you find it? You simply must tell me!'

Paz was ignoring him, looking over instead to where Tansy was having her injury bound. It looked very serious: a deep slash to her left leg. She had her eyes tight shut as Mash cleaned the blood from her fur and wrapped her leg in some of the cloth bandages they had brought with them.

'How bad is it?' Zarza asked from the doorway.

Tansy just groaned.

'Bad,' Crom said.

'She won't be able to walk very far for a good while,' added Mash.

Zarza growled in frustration. Did this mean the mission was over?

'We thank you for your help.' The farmer rabbit spoke up. He was a little brown-furred lop with timid, watery eyes. 'You're welcome to rest here until your friends recover.'

'Nobody can stay here,' Crom said. 'The Gorm will be back, maybe even tonight. You must pack your things and get your family to safety.'

'But where will we go?' The farmer's family had begun weeping again at Crom's words. 'All the warrens around here have been taken over. This farm is all we have!'

Crom stayed silent. He was being a soldier again, Podkin knew. It wasn't that the farmer's fate meant nothing to him, it was just that their mission meant more. Pod's mother, his aunt, all the rabbits back at Dark Hollow ... all the rabbits in the Five Realms. *Everything* hinged on them getting the hammer and fighting back against the Gorm. Even so, it just didn't seem fair. They had saved the farmer's life, but couldn't do anything else to help him. Unless . . .

'I know where you can go,' said Podkin. The idea had come to him the same instant he opened his mouth. 'There's a warren to the south, deep in Grimheart forest. It's called Dark Hollow, and the Gorm don't even know it's there. Your family are welcome to stay. It's warm and safe and there's food . . .'

He tailed off, realising he should perhaps have asked Crom's permission first, but the blind rabbit was nodding. 'Yes,' he said. 'You will be safe there.'

'Safe?' said the farmer, gaping. 'In Grimheart forest? Don't you know the place is full of vicious wolves? And what about the Beast? We'll be eaten in our sleep! Why would you crazy rabbits go making a home there?' His wife and the little ones squealed and tried to hide behind him.

'There's no Beast,' said Podkin, his feelings a bit hurt. 'And we haven't seen any wolves or anything. It's actually quite a nice place to live.'

Zarza spoke up next, giving the farming rabbits a steely glare from behind her mask that scared them even more. 'The forest – Grimheart, as you know it – is a good place. It belongs to Hern the Hunter. The Gorm will not want to go there if they can help it.'

Podkin raised his eyebrows in surprise. Maybe that was why they'd never seen a Gorm patrol inside the forest? It made him want to go home all the more. That, and having just thought about his mother. A huge feeling of missing her swept over him like a wave, making him blink away tears.

'I don't know about Hern scaring off the Gorm,' said Crom, 'but I grew up in the forest. I've never seen the Beast, and the wolves prowl much further in than our warren. You should definitely head there. Tansy should go back too. She can't come any further with us, and she can keep you safe on the way.'

'But you can't send me back!' Tansy shouted, her voice cracked and broken with pain. 'Who will show you the way into Applecross?'

Crom put a hand on her shoulder. 'You can describe it to us. We will manage. You've brought us this far, and fought bravely too. There's no shame in going back now.'

She hung her head, knowing Crom was right.

They couldn't slow their pace just for her. They were rushing to get to Applecross, after all. Brigid had said there'd be a little time to reach Comfrey before she either died or became Gorm, but there wouldn't be long enough to wait for Tansy to heal.

'We should send the children back too,' said Zarza. 'This is no place for them.'

Pook, still curled in Podkin's arms, took a deep breath, ready for another scream, but Crom spoke first.

'No. The children stay with us. Paz just saved all our lives, in case you hadn't noticed, and Podkin has done the same for me in the past. We need them with us. Besides, who made this *your* mission? What if we don't want you to come with us?'

Zarza laughed, as though this was the most stupid thing she'd ever heard. She was right, of course. They needed her more than anyone else. Her fighting skills were incredible.

'I'm coming too,' said Yarrow. 'I've already got three stanzas worked out about this escapade, and it's shaping up to be the song of all songs. Wild polecats couldn't drag me away.'

'I, on the other hand, think my skills might be

needed to escort this group back to your warren in the forest,' said Vetch. 'I'm no good at fighting Gorm, but I can sneak and hide well enough. I know a little healing too.'

The others didn't bat an eyelid at this, as if they expected it anyway, but it made Podkin wonder about the ginger-furred rabbit. Missing – probably hiding – when the fight was raging, jumping at the first chance to run off . . . Vetch was a coward, and a sneaky one too. *He's only trying to survive*, Podkin told himself, but it still didn't seem right. Not when the rest of them were just as frightened, yet determined to carry on.

'Very well,' said Zarza. 'The lop and Vetch will take the farmers to safety. The rest of us will push on to Applecross. We leave in five minutes.'

There were a few moans from the farmer and his family, but they mostly had to busy themselves packing whatever they could get their hands on.

Mash finished his bandaging, and fashioned a crutch for Tansy out of an old broom. She told them the secret way into Applecross with as much detail as she could manage. Podkin listened in, hoping it would be enough.

They took the chance to restock their packs from the farmer's pantry, and then – all too soon – they were outside again, ready to head off into the darkness.

Podkin made a point of not looking at whatever remained of the Gorm. From the corner of his eye he could see that the vines and tendrils had already withered and shrunk, leaving behind piles of brown leaves and rusted iron. There was a foul, metallic stink in the air that made him want to hurry away from the farm as quickly as possible.

There was only time for a brief farewell. Crom gave Tansy a hug and a gentle pat on the shoulder. Vetch tried to give everyone a limp handshake, smiling and smirking away to himself. Podkin resisted the urge to wipe his paw clean afterwards.

And then the two groups parted. One off into the Gorm-filled unknown, the other back to the deep tunnels and warm firesides of Dark Hollow. Podkin watched the others fade into the night, thinking of his mother and Brigid.

As stupid as it sounded, he half wished he'd been injured in the battle too.

CHAPTER NINE

Applecross

March, march, march. On through murky blackness, for a night that seemed as long as all time, constantly expecting more Gorm to jump out of nowhere. Every time Podkin closed his eyes, he saw Zarza lifting off that helmet again. He saw the red staring eyes, the scabs of metal eating through the fur, the poisoned veins pulsing with rusted blood. He didn't know what was more terrifying: the thought of the Gorm themselves, or that ordinary rabbits – himself, even – would be turned into those soulless monsters if nobody was able to stop them. If *he* wasn't able to stop them.

Everyone was glad when the sky began to lighten for dawn. As shades of grey began to emerge around them, they saw they were near another cluster of trees. A bigger one this time, running alongside a huge stretch of empty ground. It wasn't until the sky brightened further still that Podkin realised the emptiness was water. It was an enormous lake, reflecting the grey clouds above like a mirror.

They were safely in the woods soon after, and made their way down through the trees towards the shore. Podkin and Paz couldn't stop staring at the water. They had never seen so much of it in one place before. It stretched from the gently lapping shallows before them, all the way to the horizon.

'Mirrormoon lake,' Yarrow said. 'Once a peaceful, beautiful place. I've written several poems about it, if you would care to hear them.'

'Perhaps later,' said Crom, scowling. 'How far are we from the island?'

Podkin looked along the shore and saw, maybe a kilometre away, a rough jumble of rocks poking out of the water, topped with a shaggy carpet of grass and bramble bushes. A solitary standing stone jutted up at one end, catching the first rays of the sun.

'Not far,' he said. 'I can see it quite clearly.'

'Then we should be just north of Applecross,' said Crom. 'Keep well inside the trees, everyone.'

'What do we do now?' Podkin asked. He hoped the answer would have something to do with sleeping, and perhaps a bit of food.

'We wait for night,' said Zarza. 'And we plan our attack.'

*

Podkin slept most of the day away, or at least tried to. Paz, Pook and he lay curled amongst the roots of a tall hazel tree, looking up at the branches above. He loved the way the light shone down through the fresh green leaves, making speckled patterns as they overlapped each other, gently moving to and fro in the breeze. It was like lying on the bottom of a green pond, looking up through the ripples. As he slipped in and out of sleep he had many strange half-dreams about talking fish and swimming birds.

Later, they ate a light meal of foraged watercress

and primrose leaves that Mash had found. Crom got them to help sharpen all the spears and swords again, and Yarrow taught Pook a children's rhyme or two. It seemed like the longest day Podkin had ever known. Part of him wanted night to fall quickly, so they could get the horrid task of sneaking into Applecross over and done with, and part of him wanted to stay in this soft, quiet, green-lit woodland forever.

And through it all Zarza sat in the top branches of an oak tree, looking out towards Applecross warren. Silent and motionless, like a bird of prey waiting for its dinner. Somehow it made Podkin even more nervous.

'Will there be lots of Gorm in the warren, do you think?' he asked Paz, for the fifth or sixth time.

'I keep telling you, Podkin: I. Don't. Know. I didn't know ten minutes ago, and I still don't know now.'

'There weren't any at Redwater warren, and that had been taken over.' Podkin and Paz had run there after their own home had been invaded. The chieftain had been killed, his children kidnapped and the chief's wife turned into a Gorm agent. It was where Podkin had lost his ear, and nearly his life, trying to escape.

'There weren't,' agreed Paz. 'But they had left that horrid metal statue instead. It was part of Gormalech, I think. It helped call the Gorm when it saw us.'

'Do you think there'll be one in Applecross too? Do you think it will call the Gorm again?'

Paz took Podkin by the shoulders and pressed her forehead against his. 'Look, Pod. I know you're scared. I am too. Terrified. None of us wants to go in there – except Zarza, maybe – and we're all worried about what we might find. But we have to do it if we want to keep ourselves and Mother and every other rabbit safe. So we just have to get on with it. We probably *will* see some Gorm, and they *will* try to get us. But we've seen them before and escaped, haven't we? Besides, it's not like we're going into a Gorm-infested warren all on our own, is it? We've got two tail-kicking warriors with us, and a whole load of magical weapons. It's the Gorm who should be afraid of *us*.'

'Well said, Gift-bearer.' Zarza had come down

from her tree and walked up behind them without a sound. 'Dusk is beginning to fall. We should get ready.'

'Did you see any Gorm while you were watching the warren?' Podkin asked. The bonedancer shook her masked head.

'Two rabbits only, bringing food in from the fields. They looked normal, but sick, maybe. Weak.'

Podkin remembered Redwater again, and how the remaining rabbits were like shadows of themselves. The Gorm always left some people behind when they took over a warren, but not as free rabbits. They were slaves, made to gather food and obey their masters, never knowing when they too would be dragged off to be turned into metal-filled creatures.

'We're all ready to go.' Crom was holding a freshly sharpened spear. Two bronze swords were sheathed at his belt, and his leather armour had been carefully coated with more black polish. Mash had his blowpipe ready, the pouches on his bandoliers stuffed with darts and bullets. Yarrow had his dark green cloak wrapped around him, the deep hood covering his jewelled nose. An extra pair of eyes peeped out from its depths: Pook was in there too, clinging to the bard's neck.

Oh whiskers, Podkin thought. *This is it. We're actually going into that place.* He thought of his mother, waking up by the fireside in Dark Hollow and looking around for him. What if he never came back? Would she know what had happened to him? Would she be cross with him for leaving? Would she understand that he'd done it to keep her, and all the other rabbits, safe?

With silent prayers to their gods and goddesses, the rabbits made their way through the darkening woods towards Applecross warren.

*

They waited at the treeline until the first stars appeared in the purpling sky overhead. Podkin was pleased to see a huge white full moon rising, but then remembered that they were going into an *underground* warren. Moonfyre would be useless again.

In the sheath at his side, Starclaw gave a little shudder. *Not me, though*, it seemed to be saying. Podkin patted it, but knew that it would be useless too, if it came to a fight with the Gorm. If only it had the power to cut through their armour.

'We go,' whispered Zarza, and they headed out of cover, following the shore of the lake. Tansy had told Crom about a secret side entrance, one that should let them in to the tunnels on the outskirts of the warren, avoiding the longburrow where the Gorm were most likely to be. They made their way as quietly as they could, keeping low to the ground.

Luckily for them, rabbits didn't leave sentries outside their warrens overnight. They didn't need to – that was the whole point of being safe below the ground. It meant that the little group was able to get right up to the warren itself without having to worry about incoming spears turning them into pincushions.

Podkin had never seen a lakeside warren before. All the places he had ever visited had been in forest or woodland, where trees grew thickly above the entrance doors, their roots twirling down, in and around the burrows.

Applecross was out in the open, a huge mound of earth topped with grass and wildflowers. A ring

of stones was spaced around the base, each one carved into the likeness of a rabbit. Simple, plump-bellied and prosperous figures with smiles and huge lop ears.

They approached the warren from the back, and so couldn't see the entrance doors, but beyond the mound itself were the famous Applecross orchards. Neat rows of well-tended trees in fields fenced off with drystone walls. The lake's water kept the ground here fertile and moist, and the fruit the rabbits grew was traded throughout all of Gotland. Or at least it was, before the Gorm came.

Crom was counting the little rabbit statues, brushing them with his fingertips as Mash led him around the perimeter. '... four, five, six from the lake. This must be the one.'

The two rabbits bent and lifted the statue. It swung upwards, along with a large square of grass, revealing a tunnel into the warren beneath. Lamplight spilled out, and Podkin could see steps leading down.

This is it, he thought, as Zarza drew her sword. She was first into the warren, followed by Mash,

Crom, then Podkin and Paz. Yarrow brought up the rear, closing the trapdoor behind them.

They found themselves in a corridor, much like that of any other warren. Packed, whitewashed earth walls with little nooks for oil lamps. Paving slabs of granite and sandstone in a chequered pattern on the floor. Struts of wood supporting the roof here and there, carved with apples and pears. It was only the thought that a Gorm warrior could come striding around the corner at any moment that made it so terrifying. Podkin could feel his teeth beginning to chatter. He held a paw out in front of him and watched his fingers shake.

'It's all right,' Paz whispered into his good ear. 'I'm here with you.' And she took his trembling paw in hers, squeezing tight.

'Which way?' Zarza hissed. In the underground lamplight, her eyes were lost in the hollows of her mask. She truly looked like some kind of skeletal beast, out hunting for flesh.

'Tansy said the strongrooms were to the right and down. Cellars where they keep the cider. That's the most likely place for prisoners.'

The bonedancer nodded, and headed off that way, moving as silently as a night breeze. They all padded after, Podkin wincing at how loud his feet sounded on the paving stones below.

What if the priestess isn't in the cider cellar? His mind was racing. *What if she's dead already? What if they've taken her to a different warren to change her into a Gorm?*

Starclaw crackled with energy, sensing his fear. Podkin drew the dagger and held it out in front of him, just like Zarza with her curved blade. It made him feel better somehow.

The corridor wound around what must be the edge of the warren, sloping downwards all the time. Podkin could feel the air becoming cooler, damper (were they going beneath the lake itself? What if all that water started pouring in on them?) He hardly dared breathe, waiting for the moment when they walked into somebody coming the other way.

Eventually, of course, it happened. Padding feet on the floor ahead, and Zarza suddenly pressing herself against the wall. Crom and Mash copied her, then Paz was yanking him back too. The footsteps grew closer and the flickering shadow of a rabbit appeared on the wall before them: two wavering ears reaching out as if sensing the way ahead.

The shadow's owner was a few seconds behind it. Podkin had a glimpse of a hunched, tired-looking old lop rabbit – not Gorm, thank the Goddess – before Zarza leapt on him, crushing him against the far wall and doing something with her fingers to his throat that made him gasp and choke. His eyes bulged out of their sockets as the poor thing tried to breathe.

'If you scream, you die,' the bonedancer whispered. Judging by the look of terror on his face, the old rabbit was thinking a monster had him. *Just like I did*, Podkin thought.

'Your priestess. Is she still here?' Zarza loosened her grip on the rabbit's throat, just enough to let him croak a reply.

'Comfrey? Yes ...'

'Where?' Zarza showed the rabbit her blade. 'Quickly now. I haven't killed anything today, and it will be midnight soon.'

'In the temple!' the old rabbit croaked, squirming as far away from the sword as he could. 'Back there!'

He pointed back the way they had come, deeper into the warren. Podkin silently groaned. The deep, deserted cellars would have been so much easier.

'How many Gorm are here?' Crom asked. The old rabbit blinked up at him, probably wondering what a normal rabbit was doing invading his warren along with a skull-faced demon.

'Three soldiers, I think. They come and go. Please don't let your monster hurt me.'

'She won't, if you answer us well. Is the priestess still alive? Can she speak?'

'I ... I don't know.' The old rabbit was crying now. Podkin didn't know if he was terrified or just heartbroken by what had happened to him. 'They have her chained up with this *thing*. A lump of metal that moves and whispers. I think it's changing her into ... into one of *them*. But she's been fighting it, even though it makes them angry. I've only been in there once or twice. It's too horrible. Mostly I stay out of the way, down in the cellar.' A sudden glimmer of hope appeared in the old rabbit's face. 'Are you here to save us? Will you kill the Gorm?'

He looked at Crom, pleading, but then Zarza

twisted her hand at his throat in a certain way and his eyes snapped shut. His mouth sagged open and she let him go, watching him crumple on to the floor.

'You killed him!' Podkin was horrified.

'Not dead. Asleep.' Zarza shook her head at the little rabbit. 'I'm not a monster you know.'

There are many rabbits who would disagree with you, Podkin thought, but for once he realised it was best to keep his mouth shut.

'A whispering lump of metal,' Yarrow said. 'I've heard tell of such a thing from other rabbits.'

'Yes,' said Paz. 'We've seen them before. At Redwater and the Gorm camp. We think they're part of the Gorm's god-thing. It speaks to them somehow.'

'And it turns them into Gorm,' Podkin added. 'That's what the one at the camp was doing, anyway.'

'I could sense it,' said Crom. 'It had an evil power.'

Zarza made a gesture with her long fingers, a warding sign. 'I too have heard of this. My goddess hates these things even more than the Gorm themselves. We must be quick, and very careful.'

They left the old rabbit unconscious on the floor, and changed their direction, heading up towards

189

the temple. Podkin tightened his grip on Starclaw, remembering the writhing metal statues he had seen before and how they made his skin crawl. The Gorm were definitely trying to change the priestess into one of them. Had they arrived in time to save her?

*

The temple was usually built close to the longburrow, the heart of every warren. Applecross was no different, and they found the place easily enough, luckily without having to go through the longburrow itself. Apart from the old rabbit they had seen, the warren seemed deserted. Zarza had been stopping and listening at doors as she passed, always nodding and moving on. Could she hear rabbits inside? Or had the warren been all but emptied, the inhabitants used as slaves, shuttled off to camps like the one they had raided? Podkin stopped and listened at a door himself, but couldn't hear anything.

The temple was to Estra, the Goddess, and its entrance doors were of elaborately carved wood. Somebody had hacked and chopped at the beautiful woodwork, as if trying to destroy it, but delicate trails of looping vines and apple blossom still peeked out from the destruction. Hours of painstaking work ruined by some monster with an axe. The sight of it made Podkin sad beyond words. Take the warren's wealth and supplies maybe, but why destroy its beauty too? What could make someone so hateful and angry?

Zarza was at the temple door now, easing it open while Crom and Mash watched the corridor. Somewhere further inside the warren, voices could be heard. *Probably the longburrow*, Podkin thought, praying that whoever it was stayed where they were.

Seeing the coast was clear, Zarza slipped inside. They all followed, Podkin holding his breath, dreading what he would see.

It was everything he feared.

The temple, a place of peace, beauty and quiet worship, had been hacked apart like the doorway outside. Tapestries and statues lay slashed and ruined on the floor all around. Cruel, spiky runes had been painted everywhere in something that looked like blood.

At the far end of the temple, where the altar should stand, a rabbit had been chained to the wall, her robes ripped and bloodied, her fur matted all over with half-healed wounds. Her ears were tattered and torn, her head hanging down, body limp.

But in front of her was the worst thing. A lump of metal, just like the ones Podkin had seen before. Cold black iron – all lumps and spikes. It seemed to pulse with an evil power: greed, hatred, anger, or a soupy mix of all three. You could *feel* it seething, could smell burning iron in the back of your nose, an acid taste on your tongue.

As the rabbits entered the room, the thing twitched in response. It juddered and moved, sliding like an uncoiling snake. Waves of power spread out from it. It made Crom stagger sideways. Yarrow and Mash both gasped, and Zarza almost fell to the floor, retching and spitting.

Podkin couldn't help giving a little squeak of fear. The thing was calling out, sending a silent alarm to its Gorm slaves. It wasn't fair – they hadn't even had time to see if the priestess was still alive! Was there some way to stop it before it was too late? He slapped at the brooch, waved his dagger: neither was any good. What about Paz's sickle?

He turned to his sister. She was staring at the pillar, almost hypnotised. 'Paz!' he hissed and shook her shoulder. She came back to herself and looked down at him, dazed.

'The sickle!' Podkin said, pulling at her belt. 'Stop that thing from calling out!'

Paz quickly realised what her brother was saying. She pulled Ailfew from her belt and held it up. There were no plants here beneath the earth, but they were growing above, on the surface of the warren. Podkin watched her close her eyes and call to them, summoning them down to help.

Almost instantly, cracks began to appear in the earthen roof of the temple. Powdery soil rained down on them as roots began to push through from above. Tiny, pale tendrils at first, which thickened in the blink of an eye. They drooped down in loops and spirals, clumping together as they fell, until a whole section of ceiling gave way and a clump of twining greenery crashed on to the pillar itself.

The stuff began coiling around the metal, and Podkin could feel the toxic force of the thing dim to a dull murmur. He could see it shuddering and

193

writhing, trying to get away from the roots that were wrapping it. The plant tendrils were reacting too, shrivelling and wilting wherever they came into contact with the iron, but there were always more, spilling down through the roof in a torrent as Paz kept calling them, her eyes tight shut and Ailfew held high.

Zarza gasped in relief next to him, and Crom shook his head to clear it.

Then on the temple wall, the priestess jolted awake, sucking in air like a drowning rabbit pulled from a lake.

'She's alive!' Podkin shouted, and ran up to her, Yarrow close behind him. The chained rabbit blinked down at them, struggling against the iron shackles around her wrists and ankles.

Up close, Podkin could see just how bad a state she was in. Her skin hung loose from her bones, cuts and welts covered her fur. One eye was swollen shut, and the other was already flecked with rusted blood. The Gorm pillar had been changing her, turning her into its slave. If they had gotten here even a day later . . .

'Where . . . ? Who . . . ?' she muttered, squinting at the room around her.

'Are you Comfrey?' Podkin asked. 'Comfrey the priestess?'

'Comfrey ...' the chained rabbit whispered the name, trying to remember if it was hers. Finally she nodded, blinking away tears.

'We were sent here by Sorrel,' said Podkin, talking as quickly as he could. Paz might not be able to battle the living metal for long, and it would surely call the Gorm down on them when it was free. 'He told us about Surestrike. We need it to fight the Gorm.'

Comfrey's eye opened wide at Sorrel's name, but when she heard about the hammer she shook her head. 'No,' she whispered. 'Surestrike has to stay safe.'

'But you *must* tell us,' Podkin pleaded. 'We've risked everything to get here. Surestrike is our only chance ...'

Comfrey shook her head again, looking away from the little rabbit. She would rather die, he realised, than give away the sacred hammer. It was brave of her, but frustrating. How could he convince her to give up her secret?

'Priestess.' Yarrow spoke from behind Podkin's shoulder. 'Look across the room. We have one of the Twelve Gifts with us. Surely that is a sign from the Goddess that we can be trusted?'

'We have more than one,' said Podkin. It was too late to care if Yarrow or Zarza saw now. 'Here is Starclaw, the dagger of Munbury warren. And here is Moonfyre, the brooch of Dark Hollow.'

He held both up for Comfrey to see, and when she did, fresh tears began to spill from her eyes. Her broken mouth spread in a smile and Podkin thought he heard her whisper the words *blessed be*.

'Will you tell us?' he asked. 'Quickly, before the Gorm come?'

'Yes,' she said. 'Yes, I will. Leave the warren and head south. A hundred paces along the lakeshore, there's a cairn of rocks. Reach inside and grasp the lever. Turn it half to the right, a quarter to the left and push. The bridge will appear.'

'And where is the hammer?' Podkin asked.

'In a tomb on the island. It will only open for one of the Gifts, but you have three.' Comfrey smiled to herself. 'You have three ...'

At that moment shouts could be heard from the warren tunnels, beyond the temple door. Had the pillar managed to call its servants, or had they found the old rabbit? It didn't matter. They had to get out. Now.

Podkin looked round at Zarza and Crom to see what to do. They were both at the doorway, braced for combat should the Gorm come crashing through.

'Behind me,' Comfrey hissed, gasping out words against the pain of her wounds. 'There's a passage out . . .'

Yarrow quickly moved to the wall, pushing and tapping it with his fingers. Pook, peering out from his hood, started calling out: 'Bapple! Bapple!'

'There!' said Podkin, realising what his little brother meant. 'Press the carved apple on that pillar, Yarrow!'

The altar wall was covered in carvings, most of them smashed, but one solitary apple remained untouched. Yarrow slapped at it, and something *clunked* in the wall behind. A section of wood fell away to reveal a tunnel leading up and out.

'This way!' he called to Crom, Mash and Zarza,

and then remembered the trapped priestess. He lifted Starclaw and tried to cut through the chain on her leg. The blade bounced off without even leaving a scratch. 'Iron chains!' Podkin wailed. 'I can't cut through!'

'No time,' whispered Comfrey. 'You must go. Go.'

Her eye closed as she whispered the last word. Looking behind him, Podkin could see Paz collapsing to the temple floor. The battle with the pillar had been too much for her, and now the thing was burning through the vines that covered it, yelling out for help in waves of invisible force.

'Go, Podkin, go!'

Yarrow yelled at him, and pushed him up the tunnel. He saw Crom, jamming his spear through the temple doors to block them, and Zarza lifting Paz in her arms, and then the bard was behind him, forcing him up and out, away from Applecross and into the open night.

'Comfrey!' Podkin managed to shout – and then she was gone, his friends bundled behind him, free of the warren, the trapdoor slamming shut and the priestess sealed inside.

CHAPTER TEN

Ancients' Island

Outside, the night was calm and still. The round full moon hung heavy in the sky, looking down at a twin version of itself reflected in the black glass of the lake below. Neither of them knew, or cared, that a rabbit was being tortured and transformed somewhere beneath the ground, or that a horde of Gorm soldiers could be about to burst from the earth in a murderous rage at any minute. They just carried on, quietly shining, the same way they had done for millions of years.

Podkin and the others blinked at each other,

their eyes adjusting to the switch between lamp and moonlight.

After a few heartbeats, Podkin said, 'How long will it take them to find us?'

Crom put his ear to the warren mound, listening with his keen senses.

'They aren't in the temple yet. It'll take them a minute or two to get to the door. A couple more to break the spear, and then they have to find the doorway. We've got ten minutes, perhaps?'

'Then what are we standing here for?' Paz shouted. 'Come on! We have to get across the bridge!'

*

They ran for the lakeshore and then headed south, making for the jumbled heap of rocks that was the island, visible only as a darker patch of shadow out on the lake.

As they ran, Podkin wondered about that iron pillar in the temple. It had called the Gorm in the warren, but could it reach further afield? Could it speak to other warrens, other servants – to Scramashank himself? And just how intelligent was it? What if it could tell them exactly who had been at Applecross, and what they had been carrying?

There could be hordes of the enemy galloping out to catch them right now.

All these thoughts tumbled through his head, and at the same time he was listening for sounds of pursuit behind them. The clanking armour of Gorm riders on their terrible giant rats, or the wail of their hunting horns.

One paw in front of the other, Podkin. His father's voice sounded in his head, as it always did in times of trouble. He tried to concentrate on running, eyes on the island, but it just didn't seem to be getting any closer.

Beside him, Paz was casting nervous glances over her shoulder. Zarza was lost up ahead somewhere: just another flitting shadow in the night. Crom was sprinting, holding one of Mash's ears for guidance, and Yarrow was running as fast as he could with Pook clinging to him. The little rabbit was staring behind him at Pod and Paz, digging his pudgy fingers into the bard's neck in fright.

'If you could just . . . allow me to breathe . . . a little . . . my dear chap,' he heard the bard pant.

He was beginning to wonder if they would even reach the bridge, let alone open it, when a voice called out of the darkness.

'Here! I have found the cairn!'

They followed the shout, and found Zarza standing by a stack of granite rocks, half buried in moss and hummocks of grass. Moonlight sparkled on the tiny flecks of quartz all over the stones, and Podkin thought he could make out the lines of weathered carvings, all but worn away by time.

Paz sprinted up and started running her paws over the rocks. 'Where is the lever? I can't see a lever anywhere!'

'There's no lever here,' confirmed Zarza. 'Just old stones.'

'Look for a hole,' suggested Crom.

'Or a secret panel,' added Yarrow. 'There's always a secret panel in the stories.'

Paz began making her way round the rock pile, frantically peering into every nook and cranny. Mash joined her. In the darkness behind them, noises could be heard. Slamming doors and voices, Podkin thought. *They're coming.*

'Put Pook on the rocks,' he said to Yarrow. The bard gave him a strange look. 'He's good at finding things,' Podkin explained. 'Quickly. There isn't much time.'

Yarrow shrugged Pook from his neck and placed him on top of the cairn. With Paz and Mash scurrying around the outside, it looked like they were all playing some bizarre game of Hide-and-Seek, or King of the Warren.

As Podkin suspected, it only took Pook a few seconds to find a crack in the rocks that the others had missed. He popped a chunky arm inside and shouted, ''Ole! 'Ole!'

Podkin jumped up and, pulling Pook's arm free, slipped his own inside. It was a shallow hole, half full of cold slimy water, but there was the definite shape of a handle inside. Hard and icy, it felt like metal of some kind, and it clanked as Podkin closed his fingers around it.

'I've got the handle!' he shouted. 'How do I turn it again?'

'Half right, half left, wasn't it?' Mash said.

'No, quarter right, half left,' corrected Crom.

'Faster!' Paz shouted. 'They're coming out of the warren!'

Podkin couldn't see behind him, but he could hear raised voices and something that sounded like the clanking of armour. He wished someone would hurry up and tell him how to turn the stupid handle.

'Half right, quarter left,' said Yarrow. 'And then push.'

'Are you sure?' Podkin asked.

'Of course I'm sure! I'm a bard – I can recall everything in crystal-clear detail. It's all stored away in my memory warren.'

'Your memory what?'

'Warren, Podkin. An imaginary construction in my mind that lets me store things away in the form of everyday items. On the mantelpiece in the longburrow is a box for vital information. There's a little glass apple inside it containing the instructions for the lever: *half right, quarter left and push.*'

'Stop wittering!' Crom hissed. 'Podkin, choose

a combination and do it! They'll be on to us any minute . . .'

Podkin looked at the others. Nobody looked certain except Yarrow, who was staring at him with such intensity, he couldn't be wrong. Could he?

Goddess help us, Podkin thought, and turned the handle half right and quarter left. It moved with a squeal of metal, grudgingly at first but then easing up. He finished with a push of his paw, and the thing slid down into the slimy pool with a clunk.

Nothing happened.

Turning round to look at the warren, Podkin could see a group of rabbits spilling out from the entrance, all holding lit torches. They were beginning to split up, searching the ground for tracks. It would only be a matter of minutes before they found the trampled grass that would lead them straight to the cairn.

'Well?' Paz was looking out at the lake. 'Where's the bridge?'

'It must have been the wrong combination,' said Podkin.

'Then try again!'

Podkin shrugged at his sister. 'I can't. The handle went down into the stone.'

'So much for your imaginary warren and glass fairy apple,' Crom snapped at Yarrow.

'Have faith, Captain Grumpy,' Yarrow replied, calm and collected. 'Clarion himself gifted me with my memory. You will see.'

Even as he spoke, something began to rumble underneath their feet. A juddering that spread out into the lake, causing ripples to break its perfect surface.

'Look at the water!' Mash cried, and they all jumped down from the cairn and ran to the lakeside.

Something was moving, coming up from the riverbed. A clanking, grinding something, pushing water out of its way as it rose, stretching from the shore to the island.

'It's the bridge,' said Podkin. 'You were right, Yarrow.'

The bard nodded in a way that said *but of course*, not taking his eyes from what was happening in the water. *Probably storing that away in his memory warren too*, Podkin thought, *ready for a tale or a song in the future.*

The little rabbit also watched as the bridge rose,

one slab at a time, each piece clunking into place to form a chain of stepping stones.

'The Applecross rabbits were very clever to make this,' he said. Zarza was already jumping on to the first stone, the others close behind.

'No rabbit made this bridge,' said Yarrow. He paused to run his fingers over one stone slab, still wet from the lake and streaked with mud and weed. 'This is something from the Ancients. Before rabbits ever walked this world.'

'Who cares who made it?' said Crom. 'Let's get across it. Now!'

Podkin took the blind rabbit's hand to guide him, Yarrow scooped up Pook, and then they were hopping, slipping and leaping away from the shore and the Gorm behind them.

*

It was like jumping across the stones in the Red River, back at Munbury, when he and Paz used to spend their summers playing out in the fields and woods. Except they had never gone across the river at night, and there hadn't been any murderous, armour-clad monsters trying to kill them.

Hop, hop, hop. The stone was cold and wet beneath Podkin's paws, and more than once he slipped or skidded on some wet silt. The others were all sliding about as well. If one of them went in, there would be a splash loud enough to draw their pursuers' attention, if the clanking bridge hadn't done so already.

Zarza reached the shore first, leaping gracefully on to the island and turning with a dart in hand, ready to cover the others to safety. Crom clambered up next, cursing under his breath, and poor Podkin, who had been leading him, rubbed his arm where the big rabbit had nearly wrenched it out of its socket.

Paz skipped over the last few stones, and they all gave Yarrow a hand up, Pook hidden in the folds of his cloak again.

'I think they've seen the bridge,' Zarza said, when they were all gathered together again. She pointed back to shore, and Podkin could see two of the spiky Gorm silhouettes. They were facing the lake, and one was beckoning to another, somewhere off in the darkness.

Then the quiet night was broken with an explosion

of caws and shrieks and something went flapping and clanking up into the night sky.

'Gorm crows,' said Paz, remembering the ones she had seen before. 'They've sent for help.'

'They have crows?' Yarrow asked.

'If you can call them that,' said Paz. 'They're evil metal things. Just like the Gorm themselves. They use them to spy and send messages.'

'Can you shoot them down?' Crom asked Mash. The little rabbit had his blowpipe to his lips, but he shook his head.

'Too far away. I can't even see how many there are. Three at least, I think.'

'So there will be more Gorm on the way,' said Crom. 'We have to find the hammer quickly, and get off this island before we're trapped here.'

'Can we lower the bridge?' Podkin suggested. 'Then at least those Gorm over there won't be able to get us.'

They all had a quick look around for another rock cairn or secret handle, but there was nothing of the sort. The small island was mostly barren and empty: thin soil and patchy grass over lumps of rock, with the standing stone at one end and a mound of brambles at the other.

'We'll have to leave the bridge as it is,' said Zarza. 'It's more important to find the tomb and get inside.'

Podkin nodded. There were several torches on the far shore now, bobbing as they moved ever closer to them. They had only moments to spare.

Running again, they made their way over to the mound of brambles, figuring that nothing else on the island was large enough to be a tomb. They were right – as they got closer, they could see it was actually a circular structure of stacked stones, covered all over with stringy brambles like a mop of unkempt hair. Steps downwards had been dug at one end, leading to a granite door below ground level. They scrambled down them, coming to a halt at the entrance.

Crom ran his hands over it, then put his shoulder down and gave it a shove. It didn't budge.

'Comfrey told us a Gift would open it,' said Podkin. He fumbled at his belt for Starclaw, but Paz was there first, pressing Ailfew to the stone. Podkin felt annoyed for a moment – was he ever going to get to use one of his Gifts on this stupid mission? – and then the door clunked open with a *boom* that shook the whole island.

'Everybody in!' Crom shouted. Podkin felt someone shove him forward into pitch blackness and then there was another *boom* as the door was shut. They had sealed themselves into a lightless ancient tomb.

Chapter Eleven

The Tomb

Podkin blinked and waved a paw in front of his eyes.

Nothing.

He could hear the other rabbits around him, breathing, moving, but could see nothing at all, not even a shadow. The air was cold, damp and smelt of wet stone. He had a horrible feeling that the walls were gradually inching in to crush him, that all the air was being slowly sucked out. They were going to die down here in the blackness, leaving nothing but a pile of yellow bones for the next person who opened the tomb to discover . . .

And then someone lit a candle, and the real world sprung back all around him.

Mash was holding a cluster of little beeswax candles in one paw and a flint in the other. He lit the wick of another candle with the flame from the first, then passed it to Zarza.

With the two flickering yellow lights, the rabbits could now get a look at their surroundings.

They were in a narrow stone passage, sloping downwards beneath the island. The walls were smooth blocks of carefully cut stone, interlocking like some kind of giant puzzle, without any need for clay or mortar to hold them together. There were markings on some of the stones: spirals and zigzag patterns, and here and there figures standing. They were tall, willowy-looking creatures, with round heads and no ears. There was nothing rabbit-like about them. Podkin began to feel as if he was intruding somewhere alien; as though he was disturbing something he shouldn't.

'Where's the hammer?' Crom whispered.

'I can't see it,' Paz whispered back. Podkin had

no idea why they were speaking in hushed voices, but it seemed the right thing to do.

'We must have to go down into the tomb,' he said, as quietly as he could.

'So much for getting in and out before the Gorm get here,' said Mash. 'How are we going to escape with the hammer?'

'Can anyone swim?' Crom asked. They all shook their heads.

'Not a stroke,' said Yarrow.

'Then we'll have to fight our way out,' said Crom. 'The quicker we get Surestrike, the less Gorm there'll be.'

Podkin gulped. They had managed two Gorm before, with the help of Ailfew. Would they be able to defeat more than that? He didn't think so. Their only hope would be that Surestrike was easy to find.

*

It wasn't.

They followed the passage downwards, Mash and Zarza holding the candles high, casting long, flickering shadows across the walls.

There were more carvings as they walked, feet scraping on the dusty, gritty floor. Podkin could see scuffmarks and paw prints there – quite fresh ones. *From when Comfrey hid the hammer,* he thought. At one point they disturbed a family of fat black beetles, who ran across their path, shells glittering in the lamplight. Zarza crouched to scoop them up in her leather pouch.

'Is that in case you need something to kill?' Podkin asked.

She nodded. 'Bad things happen when I run out of beetles.'

The light danced over her mask, her eyes hidden in the shadows beneath. All this death, an ancient tomb, the strange carvings: Podkin felt a cold shiver run through his fur, wishing again for the warm hearthside at Dark Hollow and the chance to cuddle up to his mother once more.

They turned a corner, then another, and another, and it became clear that they were spiralling down into the earth. Being underground was natural for a rabbit, but only in nice earthen tunnels you could dig your way out of, if you needed to. So much stone wasn't normal, and all of them – except Crom – were gazing around with wide, nervous eyes, their ears (or ear, in Podkin's case) pricked and twitching.

Podkin thought they must have descended twenty metres or so before they came across the first trap.

Mash, out in front, stepped on something that clicked. He froze instantly. 'Oh whiskers,' he muttered.

The darts came a fraction of a second later, their mechanism perhaps damaged by thousands of years laying dormant.

Zip! Zip! They shot from hairline cracks in the wall, some too high to threaten the little dwarf rabbit, some heading straight for his head and ears.

There was a blur of movement, followed by three metallic *pings*. Podkin blinked and saw Zarza standing in front of Mash, blade drawn, candle still in one hand. At her feet were three silvery darts, bent in the middle where she had sliced them out of the air. Four more had embedded themselves in the wall where a taller rabbit's head would have been.

'Thank the Goddess,' said Mash, breathing a sigh and sagging against the chamber wall.

'Not your goddess,' said Zarza. 'Nixha did not want you to die today.' She picked up one of the darts and examined the end.

'Is it poisoned?' Paz asked. She held up her sickle to check but the blade didn't change.

'Once, maybe,' said Zarza. 'But faded now. Still. We should be very careful how we proceed.'

'Comfrey didn't say anything about *traps*,' Podkin said, feeling his stomach clench.

'She didn't have time, did she?' said Yarrow. His eyes were twinkling, as though he was enjoying this adventure. Podkin had a nasty feeling he was going to end up being remembered in a song about a brave little rabbit who got skewered in an underground tomb.

'We go carefully from now on,' said Crom. 'Everyone stay focused.'

None of them had senses like Crom, and he detected the next trap. They had just turned yet another corner when he reached out to grab Mash and Zarza, halting everyone in the tunnel.

'What is it?' Mash asked, eyes zipping all around, looking for flying darts.

Crom sniffed, slowly turning his head from side to side. 'The air is different here,' he said. 'Colder. Damper.'

Podkin sniffed too, but couldn't smell anything. He looked down at the tunnel floor and saw that Comfrey's footprints had suddenly jinked to one side, hugging the tunnel edge.

'There's something wrong with the floor there,' he said. Zarza followed his gaze and tested the ground with her paw. There was a shriek of grinding stone and a trapdoor gave way, revealing a deep hole lined with spikes underneath.

'Roasted radishes!' Mash shouted. 'This tomb is a deathtrap!'

'A good place to hide a Gift, though,' said Zarza. 'Maybe we *should* leave it here.'

'It's too important,' said Crom. 'We have to press on.'

The big rabbit pressed himself against the wall and they all started edging past the pit.

Podkin took Paz by the hand and followed the others, looking around at every stone slab as if any one could suddenly come to life and crush or spear him. What if Zarza was right? Should they just leave the hammer here? Why were they risking all these lethal traps if the Gorm were simply going to take it from them when they finally came out of the tomb?

Not for the first time, Podkin wished Brigid were with them. She would have some mystical comment about how everything was part of the Goddess's plan, how they shouldn't worry. He tried to tell himself the same thing, but it just wouldn't work. All he could think of was how important Surestrike was, and what was at stake if they lost it.

*

Two more twists downwards and they came to a dead end. A wall of stone blocked the tunnel, but they could clearly see Comfrey's paw prints leading underneath.

'Some kind of door,' said Crom, running his hands over the surface. 'But what triggers it?'

'Could that be a clue?' Yarrow said. He was pointing to faint markings on the door itself. Carvings in the granite like a pattern of dots and lines.

Crom traced them with his fingers. 'I think it's some kind of writing,' he said.

'It's not Ogham,' said Paz.

'Not Orestan runes, either,' said Zarza.

'Our troupe travelled all over the Five Realms,' said Mash, 'and I've never seen anything like it.'

Podkin didn't know how to read anything, especially not the funny dots on the door, so he kept his mouth firmly shut.

They stood scratching their ears for a few minutes, trying to puzzle it out, until Yarrow snapped his fingers. 'I think I might know! There's this chap from Hulstland, a minstrel – plays the flute so divinely – who I meet every year at the Festival of Clarion. Travels all the way by foot, would you believe. Anyway, he has this system for writing down music, like it was a recipe for blackberry jam or something. The most bizarre idea, I always thought. What's the point in training your bardic memory if you're going to use scribbles to remember things for you?'

'Will you be getting to the point any time before Bramblemas?' Crom asked, glaring.

'What? Oh yes ... the music. Well, he writes down the notes on parchment and they look just like that. All dots and little lines and things.'

'I don't mean to be rude, Yarrow,' said Paz. 'But how will that help us?'

'He means that the writing could be music!' Podkin said, seeing the bard's point. 'If he makes the right notes, the door could open!'

'Exactly, my dear child,' said Yarrow, slapping him on the back. 'See, if the first one was *do*, then that would be *la*, then *ray, ray, fa* ...'

Ignoring the strange stares from the others, Yarrow began singing a tune, reading from the door carvings as he went. It was an odd little melody, unlike any way of putting notes together Podkin had ever heard, but at the same time pleasant to listen to.

Standing in that ancient place, listening to the music of its creators, gave Podkin a strange sensation. Like a waking dream, in which he'd stepped through a doorway into another time. For a moment he forgot about the hammer and the Gorm outside and instead gazed at the carved walls around him, half expecting one of the tall, earless creatures to appear and carry on chipping spirals into the stonework.

The spell was broken by a grinding noise, as the door began to slide open. Paz threw her arms round Yarrow and squeezed him tight. 'You're a genius!' she shouted.

'Well, it has been said before, my dear,' the bard winked at her. 'Although not by me, of course.'

They all craned their necks to peer around the slowly opening doorway. Their candles were held high, so that light crept inside to reveal more of the passage – another ten metres or so – and there at the end was a small chamber with a stone table in the centre. It was the heart of the tomb, the resting place of whatever artefact or hero the Ancients thought so precious that they built all this around it. Whatever it had been, it was long gone now. Stolen, or crumbled into dust.

But in its place was something more important to Podkin and the others: it was Surestrike, the hammer of Applecross, laying on the table, softly glowing, as if *it* had been the cause of all the traps and tomb-building. The head was a beautiful bronze colour, smaller than Podkin had expected, and it was mounted on a shaft of white gleaming wood.

'We found it!' Paz shouted. 'We actually found it!'

'Not so fast,' said Podkin. 'Look at the floor.'

The dusty stone slabs carried on from where they were standing – except for the last five metres before Surestrike's chamber. In their place was a giant, hopeless, empty gap. Podkin walked to the edge and peered down. He couldn't even see the bottom. Picking up a pebble from the floor, he dropped it in, listening for an impact. There was none.

'How are we supposed to get to the hammer now?' he said. It was so cruel to be able to *see* the thing, but not reach out and grab it.

'There must be a floor that slides across,' said Paz, pointing to the passage walls. 'Look. You can see the outline there.'

The edge of a long, thin slab nestled amongst the bricks of the wall. It looked the right size to cover the bottomless pit. Fresh trickles of dust around the bottom showed where Comfrey had triggered it before, when she placed Surestrike down here.

'There must be a catch or a lever somewhere,' said Zarza. 'Everyone look for it.'

The whole group searched, pressing every brick or slab they could, but with no results. They even took Pook down from Yarrow's shoulders and made him look, hoping his uncanny luck would kick in. Even *he* couldn't find anything.

In the end, it was Podkin who spotted it: a tiny hole in the stone wall, with a faded spiral carved around it.

'This must be it!' he called, excited at first. The others all gathered round.

'Put your finger in,' said Mash.

'Blow into it,' suggested Paz.

'Can you see anything inside?' asked Crom.

Podkin tried everything, but nothing would make the stone floor slide across. He held a candle close and peered in – nothing. How were they going to make the thing work?

'It looks like a keyhole,' said Yarrow. 'Comfrey must have had a key when she came down here. It's the only explanation.'

'But she didn't say anything about a key!' Paz

kicked the wall. 'Why didn't she give it to us? At least she could have told us where it was!'

'She was being taken over by the Gorm,' said Podkin, his voice small and sad. He sat on the passage floor and wrapped his arms round his legs. 'She probably forgot about that part. She was trying her best to help us.' He thought again about how they had left her there, chained up on the wall. How he wished they could have done more to free her.

'That's it then,' said Paz. She sat down next to him and stared across at Surestrike, so close but so far out of reach. 'We came all this way for nothing.'

Zarza was still examining the walls, refusing to give up. Pook whimpered a little and climbed back up on to Yarrow's back. Crom scratched his ears, trying to think of a plan.

'Have we got rope?' he said. 'We could lasso it and pull it over.'

'No rope,' said Paz, sighing. Crom sighed as well.

'I *might* make it,' Mash said, under his breath. The other rabbits all looked at him. He had been standing at the edge of the pit, looking at the walls and measuring the distance in his head.

'Make what?' Podkin asked, suddenly hopeful.

'Make it across the hole,' said Mash. 'If I jump from wall to wall, I think I could do it.'

'What are you, small rabbit? Some kind of acrobat?' Zarza had stopped examining the walls and was staring at him as well.

'Actually, yes,' said Mash. 'My sister and I used to tour with a troupe. Firebreathers, jugglers, things like that. We were the acrobats.'

'You'd never make it back with the hammer,' said Crom. 'It would be too heavy.'

'You could throw the hammer back,' suggested Paz.

'But what if you fall?' Podkin had a sudden, horrid vision of the little acrobat spinning tail-over-ear, down into the darkness. 'There could be anything down there. Spikes, snakes, bottomless pools of water with flesh-eating leeches ...'

'Yes, thank you, Podkin.' Mash said. 'I'm quite aware of the danger. But I'm going for it. Right now.'

Before anyone could stop him, the little rabbit launched himself diagonally across the pit, aiming for the left-hand wall. He hit it with both feet, then sprang off, just like a rubber bouncing ball. Everyone held their breath as he sailed across the empty darkness below to hit the wall on the other side and bounce back again.

Boing, boing, boing. With three leaps he had cleared the pit and was rolling across the floor on the other side.

Podkin found himself leaping to his feet and cheering, along with everyone else. The shouts echoed up through the tomb and got even louder as Mash lifted Surestrike from the table and held it up to glimmer in the candlelight.

'Now,' said Crom as the cheers died down, 'we just have to get it off this island and back home before the Gorm catch us.'

CHAPTER TWELVE

Iron and Thorns

'Can you hear anything?'

They were back at the tomb's entrance, and Crom had his ears pressed to the stone, trying to pick up any sounds from outside. The others were all gathered behind him, holding their breath.

The blind warrior shook his head. 'The stone's too thick. There might be no one there, or the whole Gorm army could be waiting for us. I can't tell.'

Each rabbit looked at the other with quick,

nervous glances. Zarza had her weapon drawn, and Mash was clutching Surestrike. After his heroic leap across the pit, nobody objected to him carrying it. The question was whether he would be holding it for long, or if the Gorm on the other side of the door would be snatching it off him.

Podkin stood at the back of the group, his arms folded over his chest, scowling at the floor.

'What's the matter with you?' Paz whispered. 'We've just found Surestrike. You should be happy about that, surely?'

'Yes. I s'pose.' Podkin kept on staring at the ground.

'Well, what's wrong then? Are you scared that the Gorm are outside?'

'Of course, stupid.' Podkin flicked his ear at his sister. Why wouldn't she leave him alone?

'What else is it?' she continued. 'I can tell you're sulking about something.'

'Am not.'

'Yes, you are.'

Podkin sighed. 'You'll only say I'm being childish.'

'Probably,' said Paz. 'But tell me anyway.'

Podkin checked to see that everyone else was still busy at the door, and then whispered to his sister, 'I *am* glad we got the hammer. It's just ... well ... Pook found the bridge switch, and then you opened the tomb. Zarza stopped the darts, Crom spotted the pitfall trap, Yarrow opened the door and Mash jumped the bottomless hole.'

'Yes,' said Paz. 'That's how it happened. What's wrong with that?'

'What about *me*?' said Podkin, feeling silly and selfish as the words left his mouth. 'I haven't done anything. What's the point in me even being here?'

Paz gave him a pitying look, making him feel even worse. It was true, though. He'd been unable to use any of his Gifts since the start of the mission. And apart from those, he didn't have any special talents. In fact, all he'd done was feel scared the whole time. He felt like a useless third ear.

'Podkin, don't be silly.' Paz gave his whiskers a gentle tug. 'You've had lots of good ideas. And what about in the warren with Comfrey? You were amazing then. You got her to tell us how to get in here.'

'And then we left her behind,' said Podkin, feeling even worse.

'You don't always have to be the hero,' said Paz. 'Just being here is enough. I wouldn't have been able to come without you.'

'Really?'

'Really.' Paz gave him a hug. 'Pook either,' she added. 'We all need each other. And there's still plenty of time for being brave. We've got to get the hammer home, remember?'

Podkin did remember. There were almost certainly Gorm from Applecross outside the tomb door, and what if their crows had called more? What if Scramashank himself was out there?

Suddenly, worrying about being useful did seem very stupid. He looked back to where Crom and Zarza were ready at the doorway.

'Just open it,' Zarza was saying. 'We will have to deal with whatever is out there. They aren't going to go away, and we can't stay in here forever.'

'Is everybody ready?' Crom called. There was a

hissing sound as everyone with a weapon drew it. Somebody blew out the candles, and the tomb was black and cold again.

'Hern help us,' Crom muttered.

He opened the door.

*

It was *him*.

He was there.

The stone doorway slid sideways, showing the island, the star-filled sky, the glassy lake; all painted silver in the moonlight.

There were Gorm too: a whole horde of them, too many to count, but they blurred into the background, into a faceless lump of blades and metal.

Podkin could only see their leader. *Scramashank.* His eyes wouldn't focus on anything else. All his nightmares, all his worst fears had come true. The Gorm Lord was here. Now. Standing at the centre of his men, his arms folded across his spiked iron chest – his lopsided, twisted horns nodding slowly in satisfaction.

Podkin had seen him three times before. The first was when he invaded Munbury warren and killed his father, the second was when he burnt Boneroot to rubble, and the third was when they fought and Podkin cut off the monster's foot.

It was back again now, Podkin noticed. Not a foot so much as a gnarled lump of iron, studded all over with thorns and needles. Somehow it suited him more than any real foot had. Whatever had been natural and rabbit-like about Scramashank had long ago been devoured by his master.

'By the Goddess,' Mash whispered beside him. They had been expecting some Gorm, but not this many. Not with *him* as well.

'How many?' Crom asked.

'Too many,' said Zarza.

'I count thirty,' said Yarrow, his voice almost a squeak. *He must be more scared than us*, Podkin realised. All those stories and songs he had carefully stored away in his memory warren. What good would they be if he died? Or worse still, became Gorm? *I bet he wishes he'd written them down now, like his friend did. Or at least passed them on to somebody.*

'Is there any chance we can hold them off

long enough for the children to get to the bridge?' Crom asked.

'None,' said Zarza. She seemed very calm, considering. It was all Podkin could do to stand still and not go running back into the tomb, slamming the door behind him. What would be worse: starving to death in the pitch darkness, or being captured by Scramashank? He thought he'd prefer the tomb, if it came to it.

'Well.' Scramashank's voice, when he spoke, was as hard and cold as ever. The sound of it made Podkin's fur bristle, his stomach clench and churn. 'Look who it is. The little foot-chopping runt and his blind bodyguard. And some new friends too, I see.'

Podkin wanted to say something brave, but his voice was stuck in his throat. Instead it was Paz who shouted out.

'Let us pass, you monster! Or we'll chop something else off this time!'

There was a chorus of horrid laughter from all the Gorm. It sounded like an avalanche of metal, like a rumble of deadly thunder.

'None of you are going anywhere,' Scramashank

said, when they had finished cackling. 'But before you die, you will give me that hammer. *And* the other Gifts you are carrying.'

'We've only got my dagger,' Podkin shouted, his voice finally coming back. 'And you can have that stuck in your eyeball, you big metal ferret!'

'Oh, you have more than that,' replied Scramashank. 'I have it on good authority.'

He turned to his horde of soldiers and beckoned one forward. It walked awkwardly, with a lopsided limp. When it stood next to Scramashank, he reached across and lifted off its helmet.

Podkin gasped, and he heard Paz sob beside him. They both recognised the tortured face of the Gorm underneath. It was Comfrey, the Applecross priestess they had left behind in chains.

Except it wasn't her any more. All trace of rabbit-kind had vanished now. Metal scales flecked her torn and battered fur. She had a fierce, violent scowl on her face, and her eyes were blank and rust-red. The pillar had claimed her, and the Gorm had covered her broken body in their twisted armour. Comfrey was now one of them.

'You'll pay for that!' Podkin screamed. He felt a fury fiercer than the sun. White-hot, searing anger for Scramashank, for Gormalech – his master – but also for himself, for not saving Comfrey when he had the chance. He whipped Starclaw from his belt and shook it at the Gorm, feeling the dagger buzz with a rage that matched his own.

'Leave the leader,' Zarza said to them. 'He is mine.' And she charged, howling something in a language Podkin had never heard before.

'For Hern the Hunter!' Crom yelled, and charged as well.

'And the Goddess!' shouted Mash.

'For Munbury!' Podkin heard himself scream, Paz echoing him, and then they were all running down the slope from the tomb, towards the Gorm, weapons waving in the moonlight.

It was all over very quickly.

Zarza made for Scramashank, but there was instantly a wall of warriors in her way. She wove and danced around their blades, sending poisoned darts flying like hailstones, but couldn't break through.

Two Gorm fell, clutching at their eyes, but a third

struck her with a frantic swipe of its sword. Zarza shrieked and staggered, then was struck again with a spear. She collapsed, her grey robes puddling around her.

Crom hit the wall of Gorm a second after. He knocked one to the ground, and then parried most of the blows that followed. A sword glanced off his armour, then another and another, until finally five blades came at once. He blocked three of them, but the others pierced his leg and shoulder. Gorm dived on top of him, then, bearing him down under their weight. Podkin lost sight of him under a mound of spiked iron.

Mash didn't even get as far as that. He was readying his blowpipe to shoot, when a Gorm warrior charged him from the side, snatching him up by the ears and pulling Surestrike from his belt.

Podkin and Paz stopped running, just a metre or two from the enemy. They clutched at each other instead, staring in horror at their fallen comrades. Behind them, they could hear Pook crying in terror. Thank the Goddess that Yarrow had kept their little brother safe. For the moment, at least.

'Get them up,' ordered Scramashank.

There was a clanking of armour as the Gorm soldiers climbed off Crom. They heaved the injured warrior to his feet, Zarza too, and dragged them over to where Mash was being held. Surestrike was passed to Scramashank, who clutched it in an armoured paw, chuckling to himself with glee.

'Perhaps the most pointless show of bravery I have ever seen,' he said. 'And I have seen quite a few. Your father, for example. He died almost as quickly as you will.'

'Don't talk about him!' Podkin shouted. His voice shook with fear. Would it hurt, when it happened? Would they all suffer much?

'Yes,' agreed Scramashank. 'Enough talking. Bring me your dagger and the other Gifts. Do it now, and I'll make your deaths quick. That's more than you deserve.'

Podkin looked at Paz. Was there any way out of this? There was no Brigid with her magic this time. There was no bang-dust or secret weapons to save them. He let go of his sister and stepped towards the Gorm.

'No,' Paz whispered. Podkin heard Crom grunt from where he was being held tight, arms bent behind his back.

'It's all right,' Podkin said, sounding brave even though he was shaking in terror. 'At least this way it'll be quick.'

'Podkin,' Paz pleaded, tears running from her eyes, but he just squeezed her paw and took another step.

'Yes,' Scramashank beckoned. 'Quickly now. My master wants the Gifts. He wants the power.'

Podkin took another step. Four of the sacred Gifts, given to the enemy in one night. What would that do to the Balance? How much stronger would the Gorm become?

There must be some way to stop it happening. But how? There was no part of Scramashank that wasn't covered in iron now. Even his good foot had been clad in armour. Starclaw was useless against him.

That's not your only Gift. In a heartbeat Podkin remembered Moonfyre, pinned inside his jerkin, against his fur. He looked up to see the full moon at its zenith, gleaming down on the horrid scene below.

Podkin turned the corner of his jerkin back, letting the moonlight shine on the silver, letting the stone drink it in. Scramashank groaned when he saw it, filled with the need to possess its power.

A shadow, Podkin thought. *I need a shadow to jump through.*

He scanned the ground around him and saw nothing. All the shadows were falling to the left, away from him. Could he leap that way quickly enough? He looked at the waiting soldiers, their spear tips following his every move, twitching and ready to fly. If he ran for a shadow, he'd never make it in time.

Scramashank was staring at him with those blank red eyes, watching him come closer and closer. When he was within striking distance, the Gorm Lord began to raise his jagged iron sword.

He's going to chop me in two, Podkin realised. *He doesn't trust me enough to let me hand over Starclaw. He wants to kill me and take it from my dead body.*

'Closer,' Scramashank was whispering. 'Closer.'

Podkin gulped and took another step. His eyes

were on the ground, on the shadow of the blade as it rose higher. He couldn't reach it yet, but if he was quick . . . if he timed it just right . . .

From where Paz was standing, she could see her brother walking slowly to his death. His head was low, his eyes on the ground, and the sword of Scramashank was about to come slicing down . . .

She couldn't bear to watch, but also couldn't tear her eyes away. Should she run and drag him back? Should she brave the Gorm spears that would pierce her body if she did?

Down came the sword, whistling through the air. Podkin stared at the grass before his feet as if waiting for something, for just the right moment . . . and then, as the blade's edge was about to touch the fur on his head . . .

He vanished.

*

Swish.

The shadow of the falling sword had been quick, but Podkin was quicker. He had stepped into it, thinking of the clutch of bushes behind him, and was gone.

There was a lurch, the world shifted sideways, and suddenly he was looking down on the Gorm below, the soft darkness of brambles all about him, their little thorns jabbing into his flesh.

Not that he minded. Being jabbed by bramble thorns was a lot better than being jabbed by an iron broadsword.

He peeped out from the leaves, almost laughing out loud when he saw Scramashank shout in surprise and rage. All his Gorm warriors began to look around them, frantically trying to see where he'd gone.

All very good, and most satisfying, but what now? His friends were still captured, Paz and Pook were still in danger . . . he couldn't just sit up here in the brambles forever.

Brambles.

A vision popped into his head like a wonderful, magical bubble. A memory of him and Paz, in the graveyard outside Dark Hollow when he had first shown her Moonfyre and jumped her into the bramble bush. She was down there now, and here was another lot of brambles. Would it work again?

Were there enough shadows down there for him to use?

These were vital questions, but there was no time now. He just had to pray that it *would* work. Pray, and trust in the Goddess.

Podkin looked down at where Paz was standing. He stared at the shadow the moon was casting on the ground beside her. He focused all his attention on that patch of darkened grass and *jumped*.

Swish.

From the bramble bushes to Paz's side, in a fraction of a heartbeat. Podkin heard a shout go up from the Gorm when he flicked into view, but he was too busy grabbing tight hold of his sister. He held a picture of the bramble bushes in his head as he grasped her and jumped again ...

Swish.

Back in the brambles. This time, Paz was beside him. Down there, on the spot they had been standing in just a blink ago, three spears were sticking out of the ground, juddering from their sudden impact.

'Podkin? What—' Paz started to speak, but he slapped a paw over her mouth.

'Shh!' he hissed. 'It was the moon brooch! I jumped through the shadows, like before!'

Paz looked around her, seeing the brambles everywhere, and down below the Gorm horde with Yarrow and Pook now the only ones out of their clutches.

'Of course!' she whispered back. 'But what do we do now? They still have the others!'

Podkin pointed to the bushes that enclosed them. Thick, ancient bushes that had been here almost as long as the tomb, their roots growing through the rocks to drink the cool lake water around them.

'Use the sickle,' he said. 'Wrap the Gorm up like you did before. They can't stand it, and there's enough brambles here to capture the lot of them.'

'Yes! You genius!' Paz kissed him quickly on the forehead, then pulled Ailfew from her belt. She closed her eyes, breathed deeply a few times and then focused.

Maybe it was the ancient power in that sacred site. Maybe it was the full moon, higher and brighter than Podkin had ever seen it before. Maybe it was just that Paz was very, *very* angry ... Whatever the reason, the vines and brambles she summoned were thicker, faster and fiercer than any of those she had called so far. They tore out of the patchy earth with explosions of gritty soil and reared up like striking cobras, before lashing out to whip themselves around the Gorm.

Thwip! Thwip! They coiled about legs and arms, smacking armoured bodies into each other with clangs like bells pealing. The Gorm screamed and wailed as the living greenery touched them, as if it burnt them through their thick plating.

Podkin gasped as he watched. A forest of spiky tendrils snapping and scraping as they pinned every single warrior to the spot. Scramashank himself was wrapped over and over, from his feet to the tips of his horns: bound like a mummy with only his hateful red eyes gleaming out of the layers of thorns.

Gradually, the screaming stopped, as the brambles slowed their growth. Just the odd tendril could be seen slithering now: tightening, squeezing, crushing the air out of their prisoners until the island was covered with frozen green statues. Iron Gorm spikes jutted out next to bramble thorns. Weapons fell out of bound hands and Zarza, Mash and Crom were dropped by their captors, falling to the floor in heaps.

When he was sure every Gorm was completely trapped, Podkin tapped Paz on the shoulder. She came out of her trance with a gasp, and looked down on her work, blinking her eyes in surprise.

'There was so much,' she murmured. 'It was so *powerful.*'

'Quickly,' said Podkin. 'Before they break free.'

They hurried out of the bramble bushes, tearing their cloaks and scratching their fur, and ran down the slope from the tomb. When Pook saw them, he went crazy, shouting, 'Pod! Pod! Paz!'

Yarrow followed his gaze and cried out in surprise. Podkin thought he heard him murmuring something about 'the story of all stories' as he dashed past, but there was no time to stop and talk.

Paz ran to Crom and Zarza, ready to tend their wounds. Mash was already turning the big warrior over, rummaging in his pack for bandages.

Podkin headed for the bristling green statue that

was Scramashank. It took all his courage to walk up to him, trapped as he was, but Surestrike was still clutched in his hand, wrapped all around with brambles now.

The Gorm Lord made a kind of shrieking groan as Podkin stepped closer. His red eyes stared down with utter hatred at the small rabbit, but he didn't seem able to speak. Perhaps the brambles had wormed their way inside his mask, pushing past his lips and down into his throat. Podkin hoped so. He hoped it hurt like hell too.

'Ngggh! Nooo!' Scramashank growled.

Podkin tapped at the Gorm's outstretched hand with Starclaw. It trembled as Scramashank tried to pull it away.

I can't cut through the iron, Podkin thought. *But there might be a gap or a joint somewhere. I could squeeze Starclaw in there.*

He had cut off Scramashank's foot before, but that had been in blind panic, and over in a split second. Could he really saw through another rabbit's arm in cold blood? He didn't think so. But then again, he couldn't leave the hammer either.

Podkin looked at it again, clutched in Scramashank's hand. The head was beautifully cast bronze, sparking and glinting in response to Starclaw being near it. He dare not cut that either. What if it stopped Surestrike from working? But the shaft – that was just wood. Could he slice through that? Would the Goddess mind too much?

He decided she would mind more if the Gorm took the hammer. With a quick flick of his blade he snipped Surestrike's head free, and it fell into his hand.

'Nnnaarrgghhhh!' Scramashank screamed, his whole body trembling in fury. Podkin flinched, but then realised something. He wasn't terrified any more. His feet had stopped telling him to turn and run. Instead, he was filled with a kind of calm pride. Podkin held up Surestrike's head to where Scramashank could see it. He moved it so it twinkled in the moonlight.

'See this?' he said. 'It is mine now. I have beaten you once, and now I've done it again. I am not a "little runt". I am Podkin One-Ear. I am Podkin Moonstrider. I am Podkin the Gift-Bearer. And I'm not afraid of you any more. In fact, it is *you* who should be afraid of *me*.'

Scramashank roared at this, so loudly he began to choke. Podkin waited for him to finish.

'I am taking my friends and going now. And I'm going to cut the bridge down behind me. You can stay on this island and rot.'

And with that he went to help Paz and the others carry Crom and Zarza over to the bridge, and off Ancients' Island forever.

INTERLUDE

At some point during the story (and when the two other bards had dwindled to specks on the road ahead) the bard and Rue had packed up their lunch things, slung their packs over their shoulders and continued their walk along the backbone of the downs. All the time the bard was telling his tale, and all the time Rue was staring up at him, tripping and stumbling over lumps of flint and potholes on the path, but not wanting to miss a word.

As they reached the climax – the battle outside the tomb – the bard sat himself down on a tussock of dry grass, with Rue crouching at his feet. They were up above the rest of the world, on a crest of the downs with forests and fields spread out before them, and an endless blue sky overhead, but for Rue nothing else existed except the bard's sharp green eyes, and the pictures of Podkin and his friends inside his own head.

Now the bard finishes and takes a deep breath, stretching his back and warming his ears in the sunshine. There is a pause of a few seconds while Rue digests what he has heard, and then the questions begin again.

'Was that the end? Did they get the hammer home? What about Crom and Zarza? Did they survive? What happened next? That can't be the end!'

'Relax, relax,' says the bard. 'Keep your ears on. There's more to come, but plenty of time to tell it later.'

'Later? Why later?'

The bard points east with his staff, along the ridge of the downs. The narrow chalk path they have been following spiders along the hills' spine, and then drops down into a valley. On the other side, where the downs begin again, a ring of standing stones is silhouetted.

'See there?' says the bard. 'That's the Blackhenge. Down in the valley is the festival. We've arrived.'

Rue strains his ears and there, blown on the wind, is the jumbled sound of hundreds of voices, instruments and songs, drifting up from somewhere just out of sight. All thoughts about the story vanish for a moment and he jumps to his feet.

'You mean we're here? What are we sat around waiting for then? Let's go! Let's go!'

Rue pulls the bard to his feet and together they hurry along the path as fast as the old storyteller's aching back will let him.

*

When they are close enough to the Blackhenge to see the sun glinting on the glassy obsidian megaliths, they peer down the steep bank before them and into the valley.

Rue gasps, and the bard laughs to see his little eyes almost pop out of their sockets. He remembers the first time he saw the festival, standing beside Yarrow on this very spot and listening to his new master laugh at him. *Does everything move in circles?* he wonders to himself. *Does everything*

repeat like this, over and over throughout all time?
Standing in the spring sunshine, looking down on
the merry scene below, that doesn't seem like such
a bad thing.

There is a wide valley down there, peppered with
windblown trees and straggly hawthorns, and filled
from one end to the other with an explosion of noise
and colour.

Flags, tents, stages, banners – it is like someone
has taken a huge box of rainbow-dyed material and
thrown it up into the air, letting it land in a roly-poly,
higgledy-piggledy mess of glorious colour.

A whole town has been whipped together out of
canvas and wood. An *above ground* town, as well.
It is beyond anything Rue has ever imagined, and
he is still staring at it, his mouth slowly opening and
closing in amazement.

'See there?' says the bard. 'That's the High Bard's
stage where the contest happens. It's in the centre, so
the rest of the festival is built around it.'

Rue spots a hexagonal wooden structure, ringed
with tiers of benches and topped with streamers,
banners and flags that wave in the spring breeze.

'Then you've got the smaller stages,' continues the bard, 'for different performances all through the day. Minstrels, dancers, singers, poets, acting troupes, mimes. Most years I just end up under a bench in the mead tent.'

'What ... what's all *that*?' Rue finds his voice and points to a patchwork collection of fabric mounds that run up the opposite hill, almost to the top.

'The campsite,' says the bard. 'Lots of burrows made of cloth, sitting on top of the ground. You can rent one to stay in for the festival, if you want. If sleeping under a mead tent bench isn't good enough for you.'

'And there? And there?' Rue points to other parts of the canvas town, all crawling with rabbits, singing, shouting and chattering.

'That there is the market, and there are the food stalls. Over yonder is a circus and there is the tattoo village. That's where bards get their ears inked.'

'Can I get a tattoo? Can I?'

'No you flipping well can't,' says the bard. 'What would your mother say?'

'Come on then,' says Rue, hopping up and down on the spot. 'Let's get down there! Quick! Quick!'

'Hern's antlers,' curses the bard. 'There's no rush. It's not going anywhere.'

They begin the scramble down the hillside, Rue running ahead, then hopping back to help the bard over roots and patches of crumbling chalk. As they near the entrance – a huge gateway, flanked by two carved tree trunks in the shape of Clarion himself – the bard stops and pulls his hood low over his head again.

'Why are you doing that?' Rue stops to ask. 'Are you hiding again?'

'Never you mind,' says the bard. 'I'm just cold, that's all. Come on, in we go.'

They join the crowd of rabbits milling about the entrance. Rue is elated to see they are all bards as well. Tattooed and pierced ears, dyed and shaved fur. Some with spirals and swirls, others with zigzags, squares or diamonds. Bards from every corner of the Five Realms, with every kind of instrument imaginable slung on their backs or wrapped carefully in pouches, bags and cases. Rue spots harps, pipes, flutes, lyres and bodhrans and many other things he has no names for. Strangely shaped tubes and trumpets, leather bags with pipes sticking out, things with cranks and handles and keys all over. Do all these make music? Why has he never seen them before? He suddenly feels as though he is very small and doesn't know very much about the world.

The bard squeezes his paw, knowing exactly what he is going through. 'Keep tight hold of me,' he says. 'Don't get lost.'

They spend the day wandering through the maze of tents, stopping here and there for Rue to marvel at something else new and wonderful.

They see jugglers and firebreathers, singers and acrobats. There are puppeteers and musicians, actors and storytellers. Here and there they pause at a little stage to hear a snatch of song or catch the end of a story, but there is always more to see, and Rue is always tugging at the bard's hand to move on. All the while, the bard keeps his hood pulled low, staring at the ground and avoiding eye contact with everyone.

Rue notices, but is too excited to mention it.

At some point in the afternoon, they stop for lunch. The bard takes them over to a food stall and empties a pouch out into his paw. Currencies from countries far and wide. Rue spots coins of different sizes and metals, bone counters, clay cubes and one or two sparkling gems. The bard rifles through them with his fingers, pulls out a silver piece with a rabbit's head on one side and buys them both a pastry filled with chunks of sweet potato, fried onions and herbs. It is the most delicious thing Rue has ever tasted.

'Pasties from western Enderby,' says the bard through a mouthful of crumbs. 'There's food from all over the Five Realms here. But you have to be careful what you're choosing. Some rabbits eat stuff that'll singe the fluff off your tail when it's on its way out. These should be safe, though.'

'Aren't you hot now?' Rue asks, when his pasty is finished. 'Don't you want to take your hood off?'

'Come on,' says the bard, dodging the question. 'There's more to see before the contest.'

'A contest? What contest?' And then they are off into the crowds again, this time looking at the stalls of carved instruments on sale, and the brave rabbits having fresh patterns tattooed into their ears with ink and needle.

By early evening, Rue is starting to flag. He has seen so many new things, his little head is spinning. The bard rents a tent for them, they drop off their bags and then head for the High Bard's stage, finding seats at the very top of one of the wooden tiers. Rue snuggles into the bard's side, clutching the little wooden flute the bard bought for him like it is the most precious thing in the world.

'The contest will be starting soon,' says the bard. 'Only the best from the whole Five Realms get to perform. The winner will be chosen as the High Bard's champion and win the cup.'

'Like you did?' Rue says, yawning. 'Seven times?'

'Hush about that,' says the bard. He peers at the rabbits filling the benches around him, hoping no one heard.

'We didn't find me a master,' says Rue. 'I thought that was why we came.'

'Time for that tomorrow,' says the bard. Torches are being lit around the stage, the sky above is turning from blue to purple. 'Let's not think about that now.' He puts an arm round little Rue, as if he doesn't want to let him go, and looks down at the stage with sad green eyes.

The seats are full now, and from somewhere behind the curtains, a fanfare sounds. Four strong bard rabbits walk out on to the hexagonal stage, bearing a throne-like chair on their shoulders. On it sits an ancient figure, his grey fur faded almost all over into white. He has tired, heavy-lidded eyes and shaking hands. There are freshly dyed spirals covering his arms, loud against the pale fur. His long drooping ears are marked with faded tattoos and weighed down with huge silver discs, sparkling in the light from the torches, as does the silver ring through his nose. He nods and waves at the cheering audience.

'Is that the High Bard?' Rue asks. The bard nods. 'He has discs in his ears, just like Yarrow from your story.'

'Hmm,' agrees the bard. 'So he does.'

The throne-bearers place the High Bard at the back of the stage on a dais especially constructed for him. He says something in a weak, shaky voice, that is too quiet for Rue and the bard to hear, sitting all the way at the back and surrounded by rabbits talking and munching on cooked corn kernels.

'What's he saying?' Rue asks. 'I can't hear over all the munching!'

'He's announcing the contest,' says the bard, a faraway look in his eyes. 'He's reading the list of competitors.'

It doesn't matter that they don't hear the names. It doesn't matter that the rabbits in front insist on talking at the top of their voices and chewing corn as loudly as they possibly can. Soon Rue is lost in the performances of the competitors.

First there is a poet from Orestad, who recites a ballad about the sea. He is followed by a musician from the fens of Hulstland: a funny little rabbit with long legs, stubby ears and huge feet who plays a set of pipes made from marsh reeds.

Next up is a giant rabbit from the Thriantan coast. He sings a song in his booming language of hoots and bellows. Strange, magical music that reminds Rue of deep burrows and the wind blowing through hollow trees. No rabbit around them appears to understand the words, but they all applaud furiously when he finishes.

He is followed by a rabbit Rue recognises: the female bard they met on the downs. She tells a tale of the world when it was owned by Gormalech, the metal god of the Gorm. It is a sad, tragic story of a dead and empty place – everything on it consumed by greed – but it ends with a glimmer of hope: the Goddess, Estra, and her sister Nixha drifting through space, about to find the world and challenge Gormalech for its ownership.

Finally: the star turn, a bard from the exotic tribes of the Ice Wastes. His mane of white fur is spiked up on his head, his beard braided with bones and wooden beads, and he is dressed in wolfskins and painted leather. He starts on a rhythmic, lilting chant, accompanying himself with beats from a skin drum, but the bard notices Rue has fallen fast asleep.

The bard isn't bothered too much about hearing the Ice Waste song. Not when he has already spent two years amongst the tribes there in the past. He's also not bothered about hearing the High Bard choose his champion. Not when he remembers standing on that stage himself, waiting for the glory and applause. A part of him still misses it, he realises – misses it badly – but to think of it now would be silly. He shouldn't even be at the festival at all, not with the danger he is in.

He scoops Rue up and makes his way back to the tent, squeezing through the crowds, grateful that it is now dark and no rabbit can see his face.

*

The bard is just tucking Rue up in his cloak when the little rabbit stirs from his sleep. He blinks his eyes and looks around the inside of their rented tent, lit by a hanging oil lamp.

'You fell asleep,' says the bard. 'I brought you back to the tent.'

'I missed the contest!' Rue looks heartbroken. 'Who won in the end?'

'Who knows?' The bard shrugs. 'We'll find out tomorrow, I expect. Not that it really matters. It's the songs and stories that are important, not some silly cup.'

'I hope it was the lady bard,' says Rue. 'Then I can say I've met the High Bard's champion.'

The bard is about to make some comment about

personally winning the cup *seven turnipping times*, but remembers that he is supposed to be keeping that a secret.

'I can still hear music and laughing,' says Rue. 'Can we go back to the festival?'

'Not now,' says the bard. 'Now it's bedtime. I don't know about you, but my legs are killing me.'

'But I'm missing things . . .' Rue protests.

'They'll all be there tomorrow,' says the bard. 'There's another two days of the festival left. By the end you'll be sick of the place, trust me.'

'I'll never be sick of it,' says Rue, with the complete confidence of the very young. He looks up at the bard, who has finally pulled back his hood and is rubbing his tired, dusty eyes. 'Can you at least finish the story of Podkin? I want to know if he got the hammer back home. And what happened to Crom and Zarza. Did they die? Did anybody die?'

'What's all the obsession with dying?' says the bard. He doesn't really feel like more storytelling, but if it will get the little rabbit to sleep . . .

'Very well,' he says. 'Snuggle down and close your eyes, and I'll finish the tale.'

CHAPTER THIRTEEN

Home

P odkin and his friends reached the bridge and somehow managed to cross it, slipping and sliding all the way. On the other side, Podkin put his paw into the rock, but the handle was still hidden. Instead, he took Starclaw and began slicing the cairn to pieces.

Even though the stone was solid granite, the magic dagger chopped it up as if it were raw potato. In a few seconds, Podkin had the mechanism of the bridge exposed: metal wheels studded with teeth that locked together and turned each other. It was a beautiful, complex construction from a forgotten technology that ought to be studied and learnt from.

Podkin hacked it to bits, feeling terrible as he did so.

He was rewarded by a grinding, clunking sound, as the stones of the bridge slid back underwater to be forever hidden by the lake mud. The Gorm were trapped on the island.

'Well done, Podkin,' said Mash.

'We have to run now,' said Podkin. 'Scramashank is trapped, but there could be more Gorm on the way. If we can make it back to the woods again, we can hide there until tomorrow night.'

As silently as they could, and dragging Crom and Zarza between them, they staggered to the safety of the trees, arriving just as dawn lit the sky. While Mash and Yarrow built them a shelter, Paz and Podkin tended to the wounded.

Crom had a nasty gash on his shoulder and another at the top of his thigh. With Podkin holding the edges of the cuts together, Paz sewed them up with a curved copper needle and some thread. She slathered the wounds with cream from a little pot

Brigid had given her. Throughout the whole thing, Crom didn't make a sound: he just closed his eyes and gritted his teeth against the pain.

'You're very brave,' Podkin said to him, when it was done.

Crom put a hand to the little rabbit's face. 'Nowhere near as brave as you, my friend,' he said, before falling into an exhausted sleep. Podkin lay a blanket over him, beaming at the warrior's warm words.

Zarza's injuries were more serious. She hadn't been wearing any armour beneath her grey robes, and a sword had slashed her right across the stomach. There was also a deep spear wound just above her collarbone. Blood was oozing from this one in thick, dark pulses. Her robe was soaked with it, her fur matted.

'She's lost a lot of blood,' Paz said, peeling the robe away. 'She's barely conscious.'

Just looking at it all made Podkin feel queasy. His head suddenly seemed very hot and tingly, and he thought he might faint.

'Don't look,' Paz said, her own eyes wide with

worry. She took a new copper needle and thread from a pouch at her belt and got ready to sew the wounds up. Podkin let Paz guide his hands to pinch the gash closed, but turned his head away.

When she had finished, Paz mixed up a pain-killing draught from water and some of the herbs Brigid had given her.

'This should stop it hurting so much,' she said to Zarza, holding the clay cup to her lips.

'Thank you, sister.' Zarza's reply was barely a whisper. Podkin wondered why she was calling Paz 'sister'. Did she think she was back at her temple? He didn't know much about healing, but seeing things that weren't there didn't seem like a good sign.

They spent the day hiding under their shelter, frequently peeping from the treetops towards Applecross and Ancients' Island, checking the Gorm weren't coming for them. Paz's brambles must have taken some kind of extra power from the tomb, because nothing moved all day long.

Podkin was glad when night fell and they could be on the move again. He wanted to get as far away from the lake and that island as possible.

Then began a pattern of running and hiding that gradually took them south, back towards Dark Hollow.

Every night they would dash between copses, trying to stay out of the open. When the sky was clear, the waning moon shining down, Podkin was able to jump ahead, checking their path was free of Gorm. From shadow to shadow he strode, enabling him to cover huge distances and back in the space of seconds. Sometimes he took the others with him, one at a time, making their passage much swifter. He wished he could jump straight back to Dark Hollow, but Moonfyre wouldn't let him. Perhaps he didn't have a clear enough picture of it in his head, or maybe it was just too far out of the brooch's reach.

Several times he spotted a Gorm patrol. Two or three riders, hunched on the backs of their giant armoured rats. The beasts always had their noses to the ground, snuffling as they tried to pick up a scent. The Gorm atop them would be turning their heads slowly from side to side, those awful blank eyes trying to spot the fleeing rabbits.

Podkin had to crouch in his shadowy hiding

place, holding his breath until he saw which way the figures moved on, before leaping back to his friends and telling them to change their direction. This way they managed to stay safe. The Gorm were out hunting them, but the moon brooch made them impossible to find.

During the day they would hide away under cover of trees and bushes. Podkin sliced branches down with Starclaw, Mash and Yarrow lashed them together and Paz grew leaves and vines all over the structure, enclosing everyone in a little green cavern.

Hidden in their cocoon, they had time to rest. All the leaping Podkin was doing seemed to sap a lot of energy, and jumping with the others tired him out even more. He spent most of the day dozing, building himself up for another night of moonstriding.

Only once did the Gorm come close by: another mounted patrol that woke them with their clanking armour and the stink of burnt blood and oil that came from the giant rats themselves.

Podkin peered out from the vines and branches as the Gorm passed by, a good twenty metres away, thank the Goddess. The thought of being found, trapped within their own hiding place and with only Mash and Paz to defend them ... It was a long time before he managed to go back to sleep.

Crom began to regain his strength quite quickly, although he walked with a limp that slowed them all down. Zarza was not so lucky. She slipped in and out of consciousness, and seemed to be hovering on the very edge of living or dying. Mash and Yarrow had lashed together a wooden stretcher to pull her along on, but the dragging and bumping weren't doing her any good. Every time Paz examined her, she would shake her head. They had to get her back to Dark Hollow as quickly as possible, or they would lose her.

When they were sleeping, Zarza would often wake with a fever. Sometimes she was delirious, and called out things in a language Podkin had never heard before. On one occasion she was clear-headed, and just making quiet gasps against the pain. Paz and Podkin sat with her, giving her sips of cool lake water from their flasks and talking quietly to keep her mind busy.

'Why can't anyone be a bonedancer?' Podkin asked her. He knew it was an order only for women, but he still had visions of himself in a mask, twirling a blade and wiping out the entire Gorm army singlehandedly.

'No,' said Zarza. 'Only female rabbits. Only the strongest.'

'That's not fair,' Podkin protested, but then noticed a familiar look in Paz's eyes and quickly closed his mouth.

'Not fair, eh?' said his sister. 'Not fair? Like how girl rabbits aren't allowed to be chieftains, even if they're the oldest? How about that for unfairness, eh?'

'All right, all right,' said Podkin. 'Keep your voice down! We're supposed to be hiding from the Gorm, you know.'

'You should come to the temple,' Zarza said to Paz, her teeth gritted against a sudden pang of pain. 'You should take the trial.'

Podkin could see Paz was tempted. At least up until the mention of a trial.

'What would I have to do?' his sister asked.

'First, the new applicants have to fast for a week. No water. No food. Just prayers to the goddess Nixha.'

Paz nodded.

'Then they endure pain. Needles. Cold water. Things like that.'

Paz looked slightly less sure.

'The final trial is the hardest,' continued Zarza. 'You are put into a pit with a weasel. A giant one – twice as big as a rabbit.'

'And you have to kill it with your bare hands?' Podkin asked, enjoying the look of horror on Paz's face.

'No, not bare hands,' said Zarza. 'There are weapons on the pit floor. You can pick any one up to kill the weasel.' The bonedancer grabbed Paz's arm and pulled her close, whispering in her ear. 'When you choose, you must pick the shard of bone. Not the sword, not the club. The bone.'

'Why the bone?' Paz asked, in a tiny voice.

'Because that shows you are a chosen one. Only a true bonedancer would pick that.'

'Well, Paz?' Podkin said, trying not to giggle. 'Are you going to be a bonedancer then? Are you going to kill the giant weasel?'

'Thank you for the advice,' Paz said to Zarza,

choosing her words carefully. 'But I think my path lies with healing rather than killing.'

'A good choice,' said Zarza, closing her eyes. 'A noble choice. At least until female rabbits can be chieftains.' She managed a wink at Paz before the medicine she had drunk took effect and she drifted into an uneasy sleep.

*

By the next morning, they were in sight of Grimheart forest itself. An ocean of trees that filled the horizon and called out to Podkin to hurry home. He had never been so pleased to see something in his life.

They had to sleep the day in a cluster of gorse bushes, peeping out at the place they wanted to get back to and feeling desperately frustrated. Was their mother awake yet? Had Tansy and the farmers made it back safely? Would they get there in time for Brigid to heal Zarza?

Two Gorm patrols were spotted, sniffing around the edge of the forest. Thankfully they were far enough away to be nothing more than specks in the distance, but it made the rabbits go cautiously when they headed out, even though they wanted to just sprint for the trees.

They finally reached Grimheart in the early hours of the morning. Once the sun was up, instead of resting, they pushed on through, dying to get home, using their last bits of strength to dash over the open ground and into the trees.

The deep, dark quiet of the forest that had once given Podkin the creeps now seemed peaceful, welcoming and refreshing. It was only Yarrow who looked around with wide, nervous eyes, waiting for a wolf or the Beast to jump out at him. Perhaps Zarza would have too, but she was only barely conscious, and draped over the bard's shoulders.

Finally, *finally*, they came within sight of the familiar hill, topped with its towering Scots pine. The Dark Hollow gates were nestled in the mess of roots at the bottom.

Home.

But what was that sat outside it? Somebody had built a canvas shelter out of stitched blankets and branches. It looked like some sort of tatty circus tent.

The returning rabbits stumbled up to the shelter,

just as the familiar, stooped figure of Brigid stepped out. She stared at them for a few moments, then laughed. 'I *knew* it would be today,' she said. 'But I'm still so happy to see you!'

She rushed up to hug Paz, then Podkin, and then snatched Pook down from Crom's shoulders and swung him around. She even had a quick kiss on the cheek for Crom.

'Brigid, quick,' said Paz. 'We have a very sick rabbit here.'

'You're right,' said Brigid. 'Welcomes can wait for later.' She helped them carry Zarza into the tent, where she already had an empty bed and an arrangement of medical supplies set out next to it.

When Podkin stepped inside, he was surprised to see his mother and Auntie Olwyn lying on makeshift beds on the ground, still unconscious. Dab, the other Munbury rabbit was also there, and the comatose Redwater rabbit. Of the old lop and the two Cherrywood sables, nothing could be seen.

Brigid carried the injured bonedancer in, laid her down and started undoing her bandages to look at the wounds. She talked quietly to herself as she worked.

'We must be quick,' she muttered. 'Not much time left. Pass the honey, Paz, and the turmeric. I shall have to draw out the infection too. We'll be needing some onion paste.'

When the healer had cleaned, treated and bandaged Zarza's injuries, she started grinding up some more herbs with a stone mortar and pestle. Podkin took the chance to question her.

'Why are you out here, Brigid? What's happened in the warren? Why isn't Mother awake yet? And where's Mish and Tansy?'

'So many questions!' Brigid stopped grinding, and started to mix up some kind of potion. She smiled over at Pook, who had climbed up next to their mother for a cuddle. 'A lot has happened since you've been gone. We lost some of the other rabbits, as you can see. I'm pleased to say that these four are doing much better. I've moved them all outside for some fresh spring air. Helps the healing, you know. Their bodies are strong enough now, I think. I hope they will wake properly in the next few days.' Podkin's heart leapt at the thought.

'Mish and Tansy are out foraging,' she continued.

'Not long after you left, Tansy came back, along with some farming rabbits and that Vetch from Golden Brook.'

'What's happened?' Crom asked, sensing something in Brigid's voice.

'Now, don't you go getting all cross and fighty, Crom,' Brigid said. 'It's nothing to lose your fur over.'

'What's Vetch done?' Crom was *definitely* getting cross and fighty. Podkin took a step away from him.

'Well, he's kind of gotten himself on the council,' said Brigid. 'He said you'd have wanted it.'

'He said what?'

'And he's been telling the others that you lot aren't coming back. That the place was crawling with Gorm and much too dangerous for you to stand a chance. I told everyone not to believe him, and they didn't at first. But as the days go by . . .'

'Right.' Crom spoke through clenched teeth, in what was more of a growl than a word. And with that, he marched out of the tent, Podkin and the others scurrying after him.

*

There were no guards on the warren door, and the little party walked right in, down the corridor and into the longburrow.

The familiar war council of Dodge, Rowan and Rill were sitting at their table, except now Vetch was there also, still wrapped in his expensive cloak, half smiling and glancing nervously at the others. The council didn't notice Crom enter the chamber, and the last part of their conversation was clearly overheard.

'. . . and without the hammer there doesn't seem to be much hope, don't you think?' Vetch said. 'Perhaps we should all go our own ways? Or maybe we could find some way to work *with* the Gorm? I'm sure they'd be reasonable if they were approached in the right way . . .'

'Work with the Gorm?!' Crom's voice boomed, making the rabbits jump out of their fur. They span round to see who had shouted. The shock of seeing Podkin, Paz and the others made their eyes pop out and their mouths hang open. Vetch, especially, looked as though he had seen several ghosts at once.

'Work with the Gorm?' Crom yelled again. 'And

who said you had a right to make any decisions about this warren? Why are you even sitting on the council, you ginger-furred weasel?'

'I'm sorry ... I ... I ...' Vetch shrank into his cloak, ears flat against his head. He jumped away from the table as if it were made of red-hot iron, and visibly cowered before Crom. Podkin thought the big warrior might be about to hit Vetch. But Crom was better than that, surely? Podkin reached up to rest a paw on his arm. A moment, and then Crom covered Podkin's paw with his own, leaving Vetch to slink away un-punched. There might be talk about it another day, but for now they were finally home – things like that could wait.

The scene was interrupted by Sorrel and a crowd of other rabbits running in from all around the warren.

The huge blacksmith gasped when he saw them, then punched one huge fist against the palm of his paw. 'You're back! Goddess be praised, I knew you weren't dead! Did you get it? Did you get Surestrike?'

'Mash?' Crom said. The dwarf rabbit bowed and then drew something from the bandolier on his chest.

It was the head of the Applecross hammer, the brass glinting orange in the light from the warren lamps.

'Goddess be praised,' Sorrel said again, this time in a whisper. He went down on his knees before Mash and took the hammerhead from him, gently turning it over and over in his fingers. Podkin winced, waiting for him to start shouting about the precious wooden shaft having being chopped off, but instead was shocked to see the blacksmith break down in tears. Huge sobs of joy shook his shoulders, and he pulled Mash into a hug that nearly crushed the dwarf rabbit to a pulp.

The other rabbits cheered, and suddenly there was a crowd around them, slapping them all on the back and asking a thousand questions about what had happened. After a few minutes of shouting and babbling, Crom silenced everyone by clapping his hands together, hard.

'Enough for the moment,' he said. 'There will be time for tales and questions at the feast tonight!'

Someone called for mead and acorn cakes, and the celebrating began.

CHAPTER FOURTEEN

Gormkillers

F irst thing the next morning, all the rabbits
(at least those whose heads weren't too sore
from celebrating the night before) gathered in the
blacksmith's forge with Sorrel.

While Podkin and the others had been gone, he
had been busy sweeping, dusting and preparing the
place, waiting for their return. The forge was stoked,
the tools oiled and ready. Podkin and Paz stood
watching as the smith prepared to create the first
arrowhead with the sacred hammer of Applecross.

Tansy was helping to work the bellows, Mish

and Mash stood holding hands (as they had been ever since Mish returned from foraging to find her beloved brother alive and well), and a bleary-eyed Yarrow was propped in a corner, one hand on his forehead, trying to memorise the event for his 'epic tale' while muttering something about never drinking mead again.

Sorrel had replaced Surestrike's shaft with a plain one from another hammer. Even without the beautiful pale wood, it looked impressive. Everyone held their breath as the master smith took a pot of molten bronze from the forge and poured it into his mould. He waited for it to cool, then took the arrowhead out with tongs and laid it on the stone anvil. Surestrike was raised, sparkling in the forge light. Sorrel closed his eyes for a few seconds, his mouth moving, whispering words nobody else could hear. It seemed, for an instant, that the hammer twinkled brighter than before. Then Sorrel smiled and brought it down – almost gently, Podkin thought – to *tap, tap, tap* at the soft metal.

He hadn't really watched a smith work before, but Podkin was sure it would normally be a lot trickier than it seemed to be with Surestrike. The bronze appeared to move by itself, twisting and sharpening into shape. After only a few minutes, Sorrel held up his work to appreciative gasps from his crowd. A beautiful, deadly looking arrowhead: sleek, sharp, with twining curls of metal in the centre. It glimmered in the same way Starclaw and Ailfew did.

'It's beautiful,' said Podkin. 'Well done, Sorrel.'

'I didn't do much,' said the big rabbit. 'Surestrike speaks to the metal somehow.'

'Has it worn the hammer down much?' Paz asked, remembering the weakness of the magic Gift. Sorrel held Surestrike out for them to check. Podkin squinted at it. Did it seem a little smaller, or was that his imagination?

'It has worn down a bit,' Brigid confirmed. 'I can feel it more than see it.'

'We won't be able to make too many more,' said Sorrel. 'Not without losing Surestrike. How many do you want?'

Podkin's instincts gave him the answer. 'Three,' he said. 'Three seems right.'

'The Goddess's number,' said Brigid, squeezing his shoulder.

*

Sorrel made the arrows in the days that followed. Dandelion, the wife of the farmer they had rescued, turned out to be an expert fletcher, and she fitted them to shafts of hazel wood, with goose-feather flights. *Gormkillers*, the rabbits called them, and took turns holding them and staring at the deadly points, imagining them punching through that spiked and twisted armour, putting an end to Scramashank for good.

'All we need now is a bow to fire them with,' Podkin said to Paz one evening, as they sat together in the longburrow. Brigid gave him a knowing look, as if she was about to tell him something about the future, but then smiled and shook her head and went back to mixing her potions.

They had moved the sick rabbits back into the warren and laid them in beds near the fire. Zarza responded well to Brigid's care, and was soon sitting up in her bed, drinking all sorts of broth and concoctions to build up her strength. Even though she was safe in the warren and wrapped in bandages, she still refused to take off her mask – something that made all the other rabbits wary of her.

Podkin checked his mother regularly for signs of consciousness, but was always disappointed. Pook still slept next to her, but he spent the day with Yarrow, learning songs which he would sing over and over to their mother as he drifted off to sleep.

The little rabbits had begun to think Brigid was wrong about her waking soon. Until, that is, one morning when it was still dark. Paz came bursting into Podkin's room and shook him awake.

'What? What is it? Is it the Gorm? Are we under attack?'

'No, you rat-brained lump!' Paz shouted. 'Get up quick! Follow me!'

They dashed into the longburrow – and saw their mother raised up on a pillow, cradling Pook in her arms. She looked up at the pair of them and gave them a weak smile before they jumped on her and covered her with kisses.

'Easy now!' Brigid scolded. 'She's still weak. Give her some space!'

'Hello, my darlings,' she managed to say, but fell asleep soon after. A proper sleep this time, not the death-like trances she had been in before.

After that, she grew a little stronger each day. She was able to listen as Podkin and Paz told her of their adventures, and clap and laugh when Pook sang her his songs. Not long after she had woken, the other sick rabbits began to stir as well. Auntie Olwyn, Dab from Munbury . . . soon all of Brigid's patients were fully awake and healing.

Everything would have been blissful in the warren if it weren't for the threat of the Gorm. They were all aware of how weak they still were, and that Scramashank would be hunting them harder than ever, if he had managed to escape the island. Scouts at the forest edge saw more and more Gorm patrols, but they never seemed to enter the forest. Perhaps Zarza had been right about the protection of Hern.

Still, Podkin couldn't help worrying about what they should do next, and how they should use the arrows they had made. He tried to put it aside as a problem for another day, but it never really left his mind, and his nights were full of uneasy sleep.

Spring rolled on, and the larders filled with a variety of foods. Wild garlic, mushrooms, berries, leaves and blossoms. Clary, the guard from Munbury, also turned out to be an expert chef and mealtimes started to become a treat once more. The rabbits began to put on weight, and Clary took on kitchen assistants: Thistle and Moppet, the farmer's children and – surprisingly – Vetch.

Once Crom had calmed down, and the bad feelings over Vetch's words to the council had been forgotten, he turned out to be very keen to help, and didn't mind getting his well-groomed paws dirty. He even caught up with Podkin and Paz one mealtime to apologise.

'I really am most awfully, awfully sorry,' he kept saying, bobbing his head and blinking at them with darting eyes. Paz shrugged it off, and Podkin wasn't sure whether he meant leaving them at the farm, or suggesting to the others that they were dead. Either way, rabbits did strange things when they were scared, he supposed, and they *had* all been terrified.

'Don't worry about it, Vetch,' he said, giving

the nervous rabbit a smile. Vetch returned it, in his twitchy way, and nodded his head some more. Paz and Podkin carried on to their burrow, not noticing how Vetch's eyes lingered on them, flicking from Podkin's knife to Paz's sickle and back again.

Finally, almost a month after they had returned, Zarza announced that she was leaving. She had to head back to her temple to report on her mission, and to see if she had pleased the goddess Nixha enough to become an adept bonedancer.

To bid her farewell, they gathered outside the warren on a cool, clear evening and lit a huge bonfire. Yarrow sang songs, Mish and Mash shared out the mead they had been brewing, and they ate their fill of roasted dandelion roots, mallow leaf stew and cow parsley dumplings. Orange firelight tinged everything, fresh woodsmoke filled the air, and the stars twinkled in their constellations above.

Podkin and Paz sat either side of their mother, with their Auntie Olwyn nearby. Crom shared a log with them, and Podkin was amazed to hear him quietly humming along to the bard's songs. He pretended he hadn't noticed.

When the moon was high in the sky, Zarza stood, waiting for silence and her chance to speak. As the last of the conversation died down and all eyes were on her, she cleared her throat and began.

'I am a bonedancer. A servant of the goddess of death. We believe there is a time for all rabbits to die. Only Nixha herself knows when, and nobody can stop it.

'So, this means no mortal rabbit can "save our lives" like you field and forest creatures believe. But they can, if they wish, serve our goddess by doing her will and stopping someone from dying at the wrong time.'

Isn't that the same thing? Podkin thought, remembering to keep his mouth firmly closed for once.

'Brigid, your healer, did this for me. So did Podkin and Paz, when they saved us all from the Gorm. I owe these rabbits an honour debt, which is a great thing. I shall return to my temple tomorrow, and I shall tell them of the Dark Hollow warren and their fight against the Gorm. I shall tell them about the bravery of Podkin One-Ear and Paz Thorn-Singer.

If there is any way we sisters can help you in your fight, we will.'

It was the most Podkin had ever heard the masked rabbit say. It was met with cheers and whoops from everyone around the fire, and Podkin felt their eyes all turn to him and Paz. It made him blush underneath his fur.

When the applause had finished, and Zarza had bowed before them, he expected the singing and feasting to continue. Instead, Crom stood up and raised his arms for silence.

'Rabbits,' he said. 'I have something to say. You all know by now the story of Dark Hollow, and how it was once my home. I should even have been the chieftain here, except I gave up that right of my own free will.

'Since we have been here, we have had a council of leaders to guide us. I think that – until we find ourselves safe and secure enough to choose a proper chieftain – this should carry on. But the council needs brave new members, who can think quickly and clearly in times of danger. There are two young rabbits here who have proven they have that skill more than once in the past few days.

'Rabbits of Dark Hollow, I propose that we recognise Podkin and Paz, son and daughter of Lopkin of Munbury to the war council. What do you say?'

Podkin couldn't believe what he was hearing. He looked around the fire at his family, friends and comrades and expected them to laugh at Crom's words – to shout and argue about who would make better leaders.

Instead they began to cheer. Mish and Mash at first, then Yarrow, Sorrel, then suddenly everyone – chanting their names, clapping their paws and stamping their feet.

He felt his mother squeeze his arm and looked round to see proud tears in her eyes. Paz was looking at him too, with a huge grin on her face, as happy as he had ever seen her.

'Poddy! Paz!' Pook was shouting, and then a deep, booming voice rang out, making everyone else fall silent.

'Well, councillors?' It was Sorrel, standing by the fire and holding the Gormkiller arrows in one fist. 'What's your first command? Is it going to be to use these?'

The Dark Hollow rabbits cheered, and then, as one, stared at Podkin and Paz again. Podkin realised they were waiting for them to speak. The silence stretched on and on, the crackling of the bonfire the only sound. Even the darkness between the trees seemed to be holding its breath, listening in.

What would be their first command? Did they even have one?

There had been a tiny germ of an idea in Podkin's mind for a while now. More of a hunch than anything, and it had come from his memory of Boneroot and how all the lost and fleeing rabbits of Enderby and Gotland had gathered there together, forgetting their differences and building some kind of home. Dark Hollow was already becoming something like that, but it could be more.

'Well,' he said. 'I think ... I think we can't do much just on our own. There are too many Gorm, and we are too small, even with the Gifts and the arrows.

'But there must be other rabbits like us out there. Running and hiding, scared and lonely, like we are.

The lost, the injured, the scattered. If we could send word to them . . . if they knew to come here and join us . . . we could build an army. An army of runaways to fight the Gorm.'

Silence.

The rabbits all looked at each other. They looked at him. For a horrible moment, Podkin thought he was going to be the shortest-reigning councillor in the whole of rabbit history.

And then the cheers started again. Louder and fiercer than before. Crom picked him up and sat him on his shoulders, and the others went on cheering: 'Podkin! Podkin! Podkin!' It seemed to never end.

Their shouts rose up, out of the forest and up to the cold white face of the moon, which looked down on all of them, filling the night with a wild silver glow. Podkin looked back up at it, feeling Moonfyre tingling on his jerkin and Starclaw twitching at his side.

He looked for the face of Lupen, the first rabbit, in the moon and saw instead – or imagined he did – his father's.

He looked very proud.

CHAPTER FIFTEEN

The High Bard

Rue falls asleep just as the bard speaks the final words of the story. He starts snoring immediately, his little fingers still clasped tight around his new wooden flute.

The bard watches Rue for a few moments, then pulls the blankets up around him and tucks him in. The little mite is tired enough to sleep for a week, so he shouldn't wake while the bard pops out on his errand.

Although, now the time has come, he finds himself oddly reluctant to go. Could Rue not stay with him after all? Could he not be the little rabbit's master himself?

But . . . no. It wouldn't be safe, or fair.

The old rabbit sighs, pulls his hood down over his eyes again, and then steps out of the tent.

It is fully dark now, the tent city lit with lanterns and torches, but there is no sign of anyone going to bed. Music can be heard from every direction, tunes clashing and blending into one another. Groups of bards dance and laugh and shout from one side of the festival to the other.

The bard slips through it all, head down, making for a grand enclosure at the centre of the whole thing, near the main stage.

He comes to a wall of fabric and flagpoles, with a gap for an entrance. Two guards are blocking it, both wearing leather armour dyed in rainbow colours, and holding spears covered in ribbons. They look like extras from a play about fairies, but their spears are sharp and their faces fierce. The bard has no doubt they could skewer him in several places, probably while reciting a few stanzas about daffodils.

'No entry,' says one, as the bard approaches. 'The mead tent is the other way.'

'I wish to see the High Bard,' says the bard.

'So do half of the drunkards here,' says the second guard. 'Hop along, before we have to spoil your festival with some flesh wounds.'

'He will want to see me,' says the bard. From a pouch at his belt he produces a bone token, carved in the shape of a harp. He hands it to the first guard, who raises an eyebrow, then turns and walks into the enclosure. In a moment he is back, waving the bard through.

'Sorry about that, sir,' says the guard. 'You wouldn't believe the amount of drunken minstrels that try and get in here every night . . .'

'Oh, I probably would believe it,' says the bard. He nods to the guards and steps through.

The enclosure is a big one, with several small tents and a campfire around the edge. The rest of the High Bard's personal guard is here, playing Foxpaw by the fire, or strumming at their harps and lyres. They are made up of minstrels and performers, the bard remembers, albeit ones who could cripple anyone who gave them a bad review.

In the centre of the enclosure is a round tent made of patchwork material in every shade of colour imaginable. Another guard is on the door there, and he waves the bard through.

Inside sits a robed rabbit with a box of potions and concoctions – a healer of some kind – and, lying on a bed of cushions and silken blankets, is the High Bard himself. The bard is taken aback for a moment by how old and fragile he looks. Even older than he appeared onstage earlier. His fur hangs from his bones, his eyes are glazed with cataracts, and the skin of his ears is paper-thin. The ornate silver discs in them look as though they will tear through at any moment.

The bard goes to his bedside and kneels down, taking one of his trembling paws in his own.

'Master,' he whispers. 'Yarrow. It's me.'

The High Bard turns his head and smiles, revealing one solitary tooth left in his gums. 'Pook,' he says, his voice weak and cracked. 'Or should I call you Wulf the Wanderer?'

'Pook to you, master,' says the bard. 'Always Pook.'

'Have you come to say goodbye to me, dearest? I regret to say I'm terribly ill. For real this time, not just one of my theatricals. Such a Goddess-darned nuisance.'

'Not goodbye,' says the bard. 'Just hello. And sorry too – for leaving it so long.'

'Ah,' says Yarrow, the High Bard. 'But you have good reason for that. A little wren tells me that you're a wanted rabbit. Been telling the wrong stories to the wrong people, so I hear.'

'It's true,' says the bard, wondering just who the 'little wren' might be. 'I am in a little bit of bother. I'm trying to keep my ears low.'

'By coming to the Festival of Clarion? Hardly cloak and dagger, my dear. Who is it that hunts you? Crowskin bloodseekers? One of the Shadow Clans of Hulstland?'

'Worse than that,' says the bard, the blood draining from his ears as he thinks about it.

'Worse? Are you serious? Not … not bonedancers then?'

The bard nods.

'Clarion's castanets!' There is a moment of uncomfortable silence, then Yarrow pats the bard's hand. 'Well, I'm sure if any rabbit can outwit them, it's you. You have the luck of the Goddess, after all. And they should owe you a favour or two, after everything your family has done for them.'

'We shall see,' says the bard. He doesn't like to think about it too much, let alone discuss it. And there is the business of Rue to be taken care of, besides.

'Master, I have a favour to ask you,' he says.

'Anything,' Yarrow replies.

'I have a young rabbit with me. He is gifted. He needs a teacher.'

'A teacher? Why, he's already got one, hasn't he? I've always said you should have taken on an apprentice. You should have done it years ago! What will happen to your stories if you don't?'

'But it can't be me,' the bard protests. 'I'm in terrible danger! What would happen to Rue if . . . if . . .'

'Hush, little one,' says Yarrow, forgetting that

the bard is now an old whitefur, and he even older than that. 'Like I said: you have the luck of the Goddess. I've seen it myself. Do you really think she will have forgotten you? Your apprentice will be fine, and you will make the perfect master. Pass your stories on. Don't forget – they are my stories too. I don't want them lost like my body soon will be.'

The bard bows his head. This isn't (and yet is) what he wants to hear, but he can't argue with the word of the High Bard. Even less with the word of his old master, the rabbit who was like a father to him.

'There's a good chap,' says Yarrow, patting him on the head. 'Now, I have a favour to ask of you.'

'Anything,' murmurs the bard, wishing he had come here moons and moons ago, that the years hadn't slipped away so fast.

'I have an urge to play my harp one last time. To sing one more little ditty.' Over in the corner, the healer shakes her head violently, but Yarrow ignores her, reaching amongst the bedclothes for a small Thriantan harp. 'Will you be my audience? Like in the old days?'

'Gladly,' says the bard. 'But I'm sure you'll sing many songs yet.'

'Oh no I won't,' says Yarrow, and for a moment the bard sees a familiar twinkle in his clouded eyes. 'It's time for the final curtain, my child. I can feel it.'

The bard doesn't know what to say. He wants to tell Yarrow to put the harp down, to rest or take some medicine. Anything to keep him here a while longer.

'Don't worry, Pook.' Yarrow takes a hand from his harp strings to cup the bard's cheek for a moment. 'This is how I always wanted to go out. Singing away, like I've always done. And with you by my side. I do love you, you know.'

'I love you too,' whispers the bard, tears in his eyes.

Yarrow smiles at his pupil and clears his throat. Then, with Pook sitting at his feet, just as he did in that woodland clearing all those many years ago, the High Bard begins to sing his last song.

It is a song about Lupen, the first of all rabbits, who was placed in the moon by the Goddess to look down on the world for the rest of time. It is, the bard realises now, a song about how the dead never really leave, how there's always a piece of them still with us.

And it is beautiful.

'World-class... five stars.' Lovereading4kids
With stunning interior illustrations by David Wyatt
THE BEASTS OF GRIMHEART
KIERAN LARWOOD
WINNER – BLUE PETER BOOK AWARD

Want to know what happens next? Find out in Podkin's next adventure, *The Beasts of Grimheart*!

Podkin, Paz and Pook once again find their home under threat, but this time they are ready to fight! Podkin and the others leave for Sparrowfast to ask their uncle for the use of his magic bow. It's the one weapon that could save them all. But as they flee into the forest depths, it seems they have been betrayed . . .

And watch out for the latest
book in the Five Realms series!

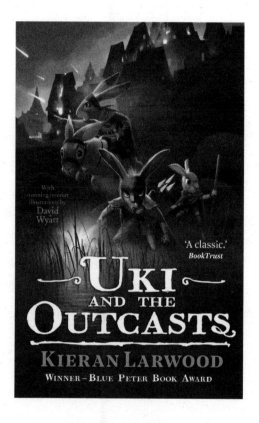

An unlikely hero must save
rabbitkind from a new
deadly threat . . .